AFRICAN WRITERS SERIES   FOUNDING EDITOR   Chinua Achebe

PETER ABRAHAMS
6 *Mine Boy*

CHINUA ACHEBE
1 *Things Fall Apart*
3 *No Longer at Ease*
16 *Arrow of God*
31 *A Man of the People*
100 *Girls at War**
120 *Beware Soul Brother†*

THOMAS AKARE
241 *The Slums*

T. M. ALUKO
11 *One Man, One Matchet*
30 *One Man, One Wife*
32 *Kinsman and Foreman*
70 *Chief, the Honourable Minister*
130 *His Worshipful Majesty*
242 *Wrong Ones in the Dock*

ELECHI AMADI
25 *The Concubine*
44 *The Great Ponds*
210 *The Slave*

I. N. C. ANIEBO
148 *The Anonymity of Sacrifice*
206 *The Journey Within*
253 *Of Wives, Talismans and the Dead**

KOFI ANYIDOHO
261 *A Harvest of Our Dreams†*

AYI KWEI ARMAH
43 *The Beautyful One Are Not Yet Born*
154 *Fragments*
155 *Why Are We So Blest?*
194 *The Healers*
218 *Two Thousand Seasons*

BEDIAKO ASARE
59 *Rebel*

KOFI AWOONOR
108 *This Earth, My Brother*
260 *Until the Morning After†*

MARIAMA BÂ
248 *So Long a Letter*

FRANCIS BEBEY
205 *The Ashanti Doll*

MONGO BETI
13 *Mission to Kala*
77 *King Lazarus*
88 *The Poor Christ of Bomba*
181 *Perpetua and the Habit of Unhappiness*
214 *Remember Ruben*

STEVE BIKO
217 *I Write What I Like§*

OKOT P'BITEK
147 *The Horn of My Love†*
193 *Hare and Hornbill**
266 *Song of Lawino & Song of Ocol‡*

YAW M. BOATENG
186 *The Return*

DENNIS BRUTUS
46 *Letters to Martha†*
115 *A Simple Lust†*
208 *Stubborn Hope†*

AMILCAR CABRAL
198 *Unity and Struggle§*

SYL CHENEY-COKER
221 *The Graveyard Also Has Teeth†*

DRISS CHRAIBI
79 *Heirs to the Past*

J. P. CLARK
50 *America, Their America§*

WILLIAM CONTON
12 *The African*

BERNARD B. DADIE
87 *Climbié*

DANIACHEW WORKU
125 *The Thirteenth Sun*

MODIKWE DIKOBE
124 *The Marabi Dance*

MBELLA SONNE DIPOKO
57 *Because of Women*
107 *Black and White in Love†*

AMU DJOLETO
41 *The Strange Man*

T. OBINKARAM ECHEWA
168 *The Land's Lord*

CYPRIAN EKWENSI
2 *Burning Grass*
5 *People of the City*
19 *Lokotown**
84 *Beautiful Feathers*
146 *Jagua Nana*
172 *Restless City**
185 *Survive the Peace*

BUCHI EMECHETA
227 *The Joys of Motherhood*

OLAUDAH EQUIANO
10 *Equiano's Travels§*

NURUDDIN FARAH
80 *From a Crooked Rib*
184 *A Naked Needle*
226 *Sweet and Sour Milk*
252 *Sardines*

MUGO GATHERU
20 *Child of Two Worlds§*

FATHY GHANEM
223 *The Man Who Lost His Shadow*

NADINE GORDIMER
177 *Some Monday for Sure**

JOE DE GRAFT
166 *Beneath the Jazz and Brass†*
264 *Muntu‡*

TAHA HUSSEIN
228 *An Egyptian Childhood*

YUSUF IDRIS
209 *The Cheapest Nights**
267 *Rings of Burnished Brass**

OBOTUNDE IJIMÈRE
18 *The Imprisonment of Obatala‡*

EDDIE IROH
189 *Forty-Eight Guns for the General*
213 *Toads of War*
255 *The Siren in the Night*

KENJO JUMBAM
231 *The White Man of God*

AUBREY KACHINGWE
24 *No Easy Task*

SAMUEL KAHIGA
158 *The Girl from Abroad*

CHEIKH HAMIDOU KANE
119 *Ambiguous Adventure*

KENNETH KAUNDA
4 *Zambia Shall Be Free§*

LEGSON KAYIRA
162 *The Detainee*

A. W. KAYPER-MENSAH
157 *The Drummer in Our Time†*

JOMO KENYATTA
219 *Facing Mount Kenya§*

ASARE KONADU
40 *A Woman in her Prime*
55 *Ordained by the Oracle*

AHMADOU KOUROUMA
239 *The Suns of Independence*

MAZISI KUNENE
211 *Emperor Shaka the Great†*
234 *Anthem of the Decades†*
235 *The Ancestors†*

ALEX LA GUMA
35 *A Walk in the Night**
110 *In the Fog of the Seasons End*
212 *Time of the Butcherbird*

HUGH LEWIN
251 *Bandiet*

TABAN LO LIYONG
69 *Fixions**
74 *Eating Chiefs**
90 *Frantz Fanon's Uneven Ribs†*

YULISA AMADU MADDY
137 *No Past, No Present, No Future*

Novels are unmarked
* Short Stories
† Poetry
‡ Plays
§ Biography/Politics

NAGUIB MAHFOUZ
225 *Children of Gebelawi*

NELSON MANDELA
123 *No Easy Walk to Freedom* §

JACK MAPANJE
236 *Of Chameleons and Gods* †

DAMBUDZO MARECHERA
207 *The House of Hunger* *
237 *Black Sunlight*

ALI A MAZRUI
97 *The Trial of Christopher Okigbo*

TOM MBOYA
81 *The Challenge of Nationhood (Speeches)* §

THOMAS MOFOLO
229 *Chaka*

DOMINIC MULAISHO
98 *The Tongue of the Dumb*
204 *The Smoke that Thunders*

JOHN MUNONYE
21 *The Only Son*
45 *Obi*
94 *Oil Man of Obange*
153 *A Dancer of Fortune*
195 *Bridge to a Wedding*

MARTHA MVUNGI
159 *Thee Solid Stones* *

MEJA MWANGI
143 *Kill Me Quick*
145 *Carcase for Hounds*
176 *Gang Down River Road*

GEORGE SIMEON MWASE
160 *Strike a Blow and Die* §

JOHN NAGENDA
262 *The Seasons of Thomas Tebo*

NGUGI WA THIONG O
7 *Weep Not Child*
17 *The River Between*
36 *A Grain of Wheat*
51 *The Black Hermit* ‡
150 *Secret Lives* *
188 *Petals of Blood*
200 *Devil on the Cross*
240 *Detained* §

NGUGI & MICERE MUGO
191 *The Trial of Dedan Kimathi* ‡

NGUGI & NGUGI WA MIRII
246 *I Will Marry When I Want* ‡

REBEKA NJAU
203 *Ripples in the Pool*

NKEM NWANKWO
67 *Danda*
173 *My Mercedes is Bigger Than Yours*

FLORA NWAPA
26 *Efuru*
56 *Idu*

S NYAMFUKUDZA
233 *The Non-Believer's Journey*

ONUORA NZEKWU
85 *Wand of Noble Wood*

OLUSEGUN OBASANJO
249 *My Commands* §

OGINGA ODINGA
38 *Not Yet Uhuru* §

GABRIEL OKARA
68 *The Voice*
183 *The Fisherman's Invocation* †

CHRISTOPHER OKIGBO
62 *Labyrinths* †

KOLE OMOTOSO
122 *The Combat*

SEMBENE OUSMANE
63 *God's Bits of Wood*
92 *The Money-Order*
175 *Xala*
250 *The Last of the Empire*

YAMBO OUOLOGUEM
99 *Bound to Violence*

FERDINANDO OYONO
29 *Houseboy*
39 *The Old Man and the Medal*

SOL T. PLAATJE
201 *Mhudi*

PEPETELA
269 *Mayombe*

R. L. PETENI
178 *Hill of Fools*

LENRIE PETERS
22 *The Second Round*
37 *Satellites* †
238 *Selected Poetry* †

MOLEFE PHETO
258 *And Night Fell* §

J. J. RABEARIVELO
167 *Translations from the Night* †

ALIFA RIFAAT
271 *Distant View of a Minaret*

MWANGI RUHENI
156 *The Minister's Daughter*

TAYEB SALIH
47 *The Wedding of Zein* *
66 *Season of Migration to the North*

STANLAKE SAMKANGE
33 *On Trial for my Country*
169 *The Mourned One*
190 *Year of the Uprising*

WILLIAMS SASSINE
199 *Wirriyamu*

KOBINA SEKYI
136 *The Blinkards* ‡

SAHLE SELLASSIE
163 *Warrior King*

FRANCIS SELORMEY
27 *The Narrow Path*

L. S. SENGHOR
71 *Nocturnes* †
180 *Prose and Poetry*

SIPHO SEPAMLA
268 *A Ride on the Whirlwind*

MONGANE SEROTE
263 *To Every Birth Its Blood*

WOLE SOYINKA
76 *The Interpreters*

TCHICAYA U TAM'SI
72 *Selected Poems* †

CAN THEMBA
104 *The Will to Die* *

REMS NNA UMEASIEGBU
61 *The Way We Lived* *

J. L. VIEIRA
202 *The Real Life of Domingos Xavier*
222 *Luuanda*

JOHN YA-OTTO
244 *Battlefront Namibia* §

ASIEDU YIRENKYI
216 *Kivuli and Other Plays* †

D. M. ZWELONKE
128 *Robben Island*

COLLECTIONS OF PROSE
9 *Modern African Prose*
14 *Quartet*
23 *The Origin of Life and Death*
48 *Not Even God is Ripe Enough*
83 *Myths and Legends of the Congo*
118 *Amadu's Bundle*
132 *Two Centuries of African English*
192 *Egyptian Short Stories*
243 *Africa South Contemporary Writings*
254 *Stories from Central and Southern Africa*
256 *Unwinding Threads*
259 *This is the Time*
270 *African Short Stories*

ANTHOLOGIES OF POETRY
8 *A Book of African Verse*
93 *A Choice of Flowers*
96 *Poems from East Africa*
106 *French African Verse*
129 *Igbo Traditional Verse*
164 *Black Poets in South Africa*
171 *Poems of Black Africa*
192 *Anthology of Swahili Poetry*
215 *Poems from Angola*
230 *Poets to the People*
257 *New Poetry from Africa*

COLLECTIONS OF PLAYS
28 *Short East African Plays*
34 *Ten One-Act Plays*
78 *Short African Plays*
127 *Nine African Plays for Radio*
165 *African Plays for Playing 1*
179 *African Plays for Playing 2*
224 *South African People's Plays*
232 *Egyptian One-Act Plays*

THE ONLY SON

John Munonye

HEINEMANN
IBADAN LONDON NAIROBI

Heinemann Educational Books Ltd
22 Bedford Square, London WC1B 3HH
P.M.B. 5205 Ibadan · P.O. Box 45314 Nairobi
EDINBURGH MELBOURNE AUCKLAND KINGSTON
HONG KONG SINGAPORE KUALA LUMPUR NEW DELHI

Heinemann Educational Books Inc.
70 Court Street, Portsmouth, New Hampshire 03801 USA

ISBN 0 435 90021 8

*This edition has been completely reset and page numbers
do not now correspond with earlier editions*

Printed and bound in Great Britain by
Richard Clay (The Chaucer Press) Ltd, Bungay, Suffolk
Set in 10/11 Intertype Times

the only son of his mother
and she was a widow.
LUKE VII, 12

ONE

Her steps were quick and forceful and her face was cloudy, like of one on an errand of grief. She was returning from Nade.

The evening before, Oji had sent word that she should see him in the morning, without fail. She left her house at the onset of dawn. The chickens were coming out of the pen and then the palm of the hand was only faintly visible. That was early enough, she had told herself. And yet, when she arrived she did not find Oji in; she had to wait there for hours. To add to her annoyance, Oji had nothing important or interesting to talk about. He only wanted her to re-marry. And leave her son, Nnanna, to whom? Oji could not answer.

The shadow was almost at her feet when Chiaku reached the entrance door of her house. 'My only consolation,' said she aloud, to herself, 'is that I packed the basket in the night in readiness for market. As if I knew what would happen! It remains to collect some pepper, which I asked Nnanna to do for me.'

She stepped in.

'Is Nnanna in the house?' She called twice before he answered:

'I'm here!'

'Where?'

'Behind the compound. I'm collecting the pepper.'

'You're still at it?' she queried.

'I've finished. I was about to go in when you called.'

Soon after, he too came in, bringing a small basket which was half-filled with pepper. There were green capsules and there were pink ones, most of them beautifully spotted.

'That's plenty,' she commented. Her face brightened. 'How much will it fetch us?' She took the basket from him. With her right hand she scooped up some capsules, held them away from her and studied them critically. 'They are big and ripe,' she said; 'they will fetch us ten heads of cowrie shells, or even

1

more. Thank you, my son. I must set out at once so that I can sell all I have in the basket.'

'We won't eat lunch?'

'Cook for yourself and eat. Oji's wife, Nwanebe, gave me breakfast. That will carry me till supper. Come now, help your mother to take out the basket from the room.'

They brought the basket out. It was a fairly big one. A pot of palm oil, of the red and fresh, edible type, stood on a pad at one end. At the other end, balancing the weight of the oil, was a heap of cocoyams. Between these two principal items were a bunch of ripe bananas, a small quantity of okro, coconut fruits, and a small basket filled with palm kernel. There was a small space at the middle, between okro and coconuts. When they had put down the basket Chiaku placed the pepper in this space and covered it with broad green leaves. She said:

'You will please peel cocoyams for supper and fetch firewood before I return.'

His face dulled. He scratched his head and objected: 'We will hunt today. I won't have time for any other thing.'

'Hunt for your head!' she replied. 'See that you peel the yams and fetch firewood. You hear me?'

'I will not have time for that,' he objected again, his voice rising.

'May your mouth be sealed rather than utter those words again!' she shouted. 'I have a son of your age and yet I have to do everything myself.'

'I've told you, I must go out to hunt,' he reaffirmed.

'Villain!' she thundered. 'I suffer because of you and yet you refuse to do anything in the house. The mother who brought you into this world does not get anything from you in return! Let me tell you, Nnanna, you are not behaving at all well.'

'Did I ask anybody to bring me into the world?' he said light-heartedly.

'That's enough now!'

He paused. 'All right, I'll peel the cocoyams and fetch the firewood, but I must go out to hunt after that.'

Silent, she inspected the basket once more. She shook it gently to satisfy herself that the contents would not move. She said, in a commanding tone: 'Help me to lift it.'

They lifted the basket slowly, steadily. He stiffened and ex-

2

erted himself to the full. She bent her knees, one lower than the other, and received the weight on her head.

'You've started me off badly, you and Oji,' she complained. 'I shouldn't be surprised if nobody so much as approached my shed in the market today. Look after the house.'

'Go well.'

'By the way, whom do you say you're going to hunt with?'

'Ibe.'

'Which Ibe?'

'Idimogu's.'

'Is he in town?'

'Yes.'

She began to leave. 'Remember to keep clear of Amanze's house. Avoid both him and his wives.'

Evening had started. A mild wind blew. The trees around returned a slow, gentle rustle. Adagu and Obieke escaped from the compound and ran towards the familiar sandy shade a good distance from the entrance door. All the afternoon they had been confined within, alone, in the fearful quiet of the wooded surroundings. 'The beautiful artist is hiding in the bush outside waiting for small children on whom to do his work,' their father had warned, seriously. 'So please stay in and don't go out.' The beautiful artist was small-pox. The epidemic had recently ravaged the area, leaving its fingerprints on those of its victims lucky enough to have survived. Its fear still hung like a rain cloud, especially in the minds of the children. But for Adagu and Obieke, the temptation offered now by a cool evening breeze was stronger than that fear. As they ran they looked cautiously left and right. They saw nobody – no artist.

As soon as they got to the shade they began to play.

'Let's bury our bodies in the sand so that nobody will see us,' Adagu proposed. She threw handfuls here and there.

'I agree.'

They buried the greater part of their bodies. After some time Obieke said:

'Let's not hide any longer. Let's sit up and play.'

They sat up facing each other. With the two hands they each lifted a good quantity of sand and let the dry brown particles rain down in jets from between the fingers. 'Rain is

3

falling, is falling, is falling; rain is falling,' they sang in a low voice.

Obieke proposed: 'We shall now build a house and cook inside it.'

Adagu nodded absently, her eyes concentrated on the jets of sand, her body all brown. 'Nobody can equal me in it,' she said, communing with the dust.

'Stop it now and let's build a house,' Obieke ordered.

Reluctantly, she threw away all the sand in her hands. She ran her right wrist under her nose. 'Obieke, see, I have stopped. Let's begin to build the house. I shall cook for you inside it when we finish – cook as Mother does.' She paused. 'Obieke, you are my husband,' she told her half-brother, and then ran her wrist under her nose once more.

A few minutes later they had assembled enough dry sticks and broad green leaves for the house. It remained to gather the condiments and utensils for the food. Adagu went for them. On her return she brought a variety of green leaves, some palm-nuts, a broken pot and a piece of stick. Inside the house which Obieke had already completed she put down the pot. Then with her left hand she shovelled a good quantity of sand into the pot.

'No water?' Obieke queried and supplied all the saliva he could spare. He spat straight into the pot. Adagu added some. Then they both began to stir with short sticks.

A tall plant in the bush behind shook and the leaves rustled violently. They stood up in fear. The noise came again. Then they heard:

'Caw – caw – caw – w – w!'

Obieke, aged five, was ready to run away. Adagu, younger by a few months, moved to his side and held his hand.

'Hm – m – m!' the voice cried. 'I am a brother to the artist. I want to work on you two children.'

She broke into a cry. He hushed her. They stepped sideways.

'Don't move!' the voice ordered. 'I am also a spirit. I shall chew your heads now. Caw – caw – caw – w – w!' It sounded like that unearthly falsetto with which, from the stories told, children had always associated the worst type of fairies – the red-clawed, red-headed, child-eating goblin.

They took to their heels.

'Come back, pot-bellied Obieke,' said the voice. 'And Adagu with very big eyes.'

They turned. It was Nnanna. He was lying flat on his stomach close to the house, the one they had abandoned in their fright. Then from the bush another came out. They also recognized this one.

Panting, they both began to return to the spot.

'Good for you,' Nnanna jeered, grinning. 'You thought I was the artist.' He punched playfully at the broad green leaves that were the roof of the house. 'Or a spirit.' He punched again.

They greeted him with curse-words. 'Father will hear about it,' whined Adagu. 'You and your mother will suffer today. You know what happened to you the last time you beat me.'

Nnanna sprang up furiously from the ground. He kicked at the rest of the house, wiping out the product of so much industry. He overturned the pot and spilled the contents. Then, as if still not sufficiently avenged, he lifted the pot and dropped it hard on the ground.

'Repeat what you've just said,' he dared.

Ibe stood and watched.

'We will report you to Father,' Obieke said. His eyes were flooded with tears. 'You will suffer today, you and your short mother.'

At once Nnanna caught him and hit him on the lips, pushing him down on the ground. He moved on to Adagu, pinched her left cheek and twisted her ears and her lips. 'Go now and bring your father and mothers,' he jeered in reply to their cries of pain and protest.

'Let's go away, Nnanna,' Ibe said. 'Leave those small things.'

They disappeared again into the bush where they had been hunting for rats and squirrels. Hunting was second nature to them.

TWO

There was great to-do in Amanze's house that night. Amanze was the father of the two children, Adagu and Obieke. He had just returned after a round of the five palms he tapped for wine when the two wives came in, each with a child in hand and anger on her face. Before he could put down the climbing rope and the tapping knife, they had already started to say something about Nnanna being the bane of mothers. 'He nearly tore off my daughter's ears,' shouted Adagu's mother, as if to a deaf ear. 'He crushed the boy's shoulder blade,' cried out the other. They wanted prompt reprisals. Amanze sent for Chiaku.

As soon as she arrived he began:

'I suppose you know why I want you.'

Even in the dim light of the palm-fibre candle, Chiaku could notice that he was wide-eyed. She allowed an interval before she answered:

'I've no idea. I've just returned from market.'

'That abomination of a son wanted to kill my child!' broke in Obieke's mother, eyes on the roof.

'It was his mother that sent him,' responded Adagu's mother. 'They will show me their strength tonight – here in this house.'

'Well, Chiaku, it's about Nnanna again,' Amanze continued.

Just as I had feared! she said to herself. What has he done this time? Nnanna, you will betray me one day! You will betray Ejimadu's daughter!

'Please, what has he done now?' she asked.

'What has he done!' repeated Amanze irritably. 'Haven't you seen these children here? Look at Obieke's lips.' He brought the candle closer. 'See it. I've been appealing to you to do something about that boy. Please get a good priest-doctor to look into his head.'

Disappointed, she stared at him with manly self-possession.

That this should have come from an adult, much less from an uncle!

'You know, Amanze, you always speak about Nnanna as if he is not your own child,' said she. 'Don't forget that he is your late brother's son and therefore your own flesh and blood.'

'Dare you talk to me like that?' he objected and regarded her sternly. 'Do you forget that you are a woman?'

'Look at Obieke's mouth,' interrupted Obieke's mother. 'And yet she has the courage to say such things!'

At that, Chiaku lost her temper. 'It's hatred and nothing else,' she accused. 'The least offence Nnanna commits is drummed about all over Umudiobia of ten villages and two.'

'With your dirty mouth you say such things, woman?' said Adagu's mother. 'I can now see you've no shame in you. Whatever happens, I must not allow you and that evil son of yours to touch Adagu again. Of course, it's all Amanze's fault.' She bit her lower lip and shook her head with much bitterness. 'Amanze pampers you and gives you the courage to behave the way you do.' She paused for a brief while, for breath. Unlike Obieke's mother she always called him by his first name. She did so out of reciprocal slight. It was common knowledge that Amanze much preferred Obieke's mother to whom he gave the praise-name Obidia (The Husband's Heart). Apart from other things, Obidia had three boys and a girl, whereas Adagu's mother, his first wife, had only a girl.

'And yet he calls himself a man,' she continued. 'Believe me, there's not much male in you, Amanze.' She shook her head again and turned her back contemptuously. Her nickname was Fire (That Burnt her Husband). 'You are more female than any woman in the whole of Umudiobia of ten villages and two.'

Amanze's teeth creaked. 'I'll strangle that boy one of these days!' he exclaimed.

'I'm sure you would!' Chiaku retorted. 'But who will give you the chance?'

He was silent. It seemed he had been hushed by a sense of guilt, the realization that he had uttered an abomination. His teeth creaked again and his left fingers began to play on his forehead.

'Ojukwu of Umudiobia will not allow you to do such a

7

thing,' she pursued, shouting. 'If strangle you must, then you
had better strangle your own children and leave off your late
brother's.'

'He will see!' said he, for want of something better.

Her eyes brimmed. She tied her cloth firmly to her waist in
readiness for whatever her coming speech might bring.
Then:

'Since Okafo died you and your wives have been treating his
son like a stranger, even like a slave. You are afraid he may
grow up one day to demand from you all his father's land and
other things which you have grabbed. That's why you treat us
the way you do. Only a few days ago you nearly beat the life
out of him, just because—'

'Shut up your mouth now, woman!' he roared.

'You can kill me in the end if you like, but allow me now to
tell you and your wives your evil deeds and designs. Let me
ease my heart before you strangle me too.'

'Oh, it seems you have been carrying some load in your heart
all these years! Go on then, let's hear you.'

'Yes, let me say out everything this night.' She began to
speak, at long last unburdening her heart. Okafo was the elder
of two brothers. When he died almost thirteen years back,
Nnanna was barely six months old and she herself only eighteen. Since that time she had been solely responsible for the
boy's upbringing; she had had to scratch the infertile portions
of land which Amanze assigned her. How many times now had
she appealed to him for more and better land? Each time he
would merely remind her that the son was yet a child and that
she herself was a woman, a stranger in the family. She had been
repressing her feelings, repressing the urge to let it out of her
heart. She could no longer do so; she was telling him everything plainly tonight. Just a few days before, it had come to her
lips but she had managed to push it back into her heart. That
was the day Amanze confiscated the pods which Nnanna
plucked from the old kolatree – the one that stood within the
crumbling compound walls where she and her son lived. Was it
not within those walls that both he and Okafo were born and
reared? By custom, everything there, including the tree belonged to the first son, and Nnanna had a right to his late
father's property. It was this tree, with its big pods and eagle-

white nuts, of a rare pedigree, that Amanze had seized too, threatening that he would skin Nnanna alive if he climbed it again. With his own mouth Amanze did say such a thing! And today he would strangle the boy. Just because Nnanna touched his brother and sister.

She sighed and turned her face away from him.

'Is that the nonsense you've come here to vomit, Chiaku?' asked Amanze, seemingly unmoved.

'You call it nonsense?'

'Out from here before an oil-bean pod explodes on your head!'

'Let's now return to what her son did to the children,' Obidia calmly reminded them. Adagu's mother shouted 'Wajah wajah!' a number of times, mimicking Chiaku's voice.

She was infuriated all the more. 'You and your wives hate to see Nnanna grow up! That's the simple truth.' Her voice rang shrill and clear in the still, early night.

'Truth?' asked Amanze with great vehemence and sprang up, as if startled. There was a lot of it in that accusation, in spite of her wild voice and gestures. Its bitter sting injured his heart and left his mind confused. Up and down he strode, scratching his head painfully. Then he looked up and his eyes caught the shredded and dry fly-whisk on the bamboo rafter. He drew it out, swung round, exploded it on Chiaku's head – all in a fraction of a second.

'They've sent for me to kill me tonight!' she cried. Then she leapt for the small wooden mortar near Amanze's foot. But he seized it before she could get there.

'Kill me today!' she gasped. And falling on Obidia, she tore her unplaited hair, biting and clawing. She was a very strong woman, well-built too, although smallish in stature; and she was full of determination.

Amanze came at her again with the fly-whisk. Adagu's mother made to advance.

'Leave her now or I'll shoot!'

Even in the heat and confusion of the fight, they all recognized the voice. Turning, they saw Nnanna at the door. His feet were astride and the arrow was set on the bow ready to fly. 'Leave her now or I'll pierce your stomach with this arrow,' Nnanna demanded again.

The fighters drew apart. Amanze stood still and gazed in silence. Adagu's mother held her hands by her sides. They knew the boy's capabilities. Nnanna rarely shot and missed. Only recently, he took a bush fowl with his arrow, piercing one of the wings as the bird flew. On that day nearly all the children in the vicinity flocked to Chiaku's house to see the arrow that had caught a bird in flight and to touch the hand that aimed successfully at things that moved in the air. That weapon now in his hand had made him famous among his age-grade in most of Umudiobia of ten villages and two. Obidia too was well aware of the fact. But she could not bear her wounded pride. She hit Chiaku on the face with her loosely-clenched fingers and raked her nails across the woman's cheek.

Nnanna shot the arrow, aiming low. The weapon landed on Obidia's left calf and brought her down on the ground.

'Don't shoot again!' Amanze cried, both his hands up in a pleading gesture ...

Chiaku walked out of the house free and safe. 'Heart of the mother!' sang she in a frenzy of joy, her hands raised skyward in prayer. 'My many in one! His mother's hero!' In such short, broken phrases she continued to praise him until they reached home.

The house in which they lived was a good distance away, in the ancestral compound which belonged, by inheritance, to the first son in the lineage. The red-mud compound walls had begun to crumble with neglect and were covered in places by lichen and creepers. The house itself was a shanty with a leaky reed roof and mud-and-wattle walls.

Back there they sat in the open yard, he twanging at the bow-string playfully, the arrows close by his side; she brooding. The night was dark and the air was still. Chiaku's mind went back to her better years within those walls. Once, she had lived with a husband who was full of kindness and humour. He was young and energetic. He tilled the ground faster than most men did, and tapped a dozen palm-trees three times a day. Okafo loved her and she loved him. So much that gossips said she had emptied something into his soup. Good things do not last long! Hardly two years after their marriage, and six moons after Nnanna was born, Okafo dropped from one of the palm-trees, and out of her life, leaving her, a teenage mother, to fend for both herself and the child. Since then she had held on in the house in the hope that the son would grow up one day and continue the lineage, build up the homestead and keep open and in a good state the approach to it. That hope was being proved false: Amanze would not have it so. Why then should she continue to stay? What could she do in Umudiobia? Chiaku felt a sense of being encompassed by danger. Even the familiar shrill sounds of insects irked her this night and every distant noise seemed to her like the echo of her sorrows in Umudiobia.

'What are you doing there, Mother?' he asked.

She wrenched her mind with a sigh. 'Nothing, his mother's hero,' said she. 'Let's go in and cook supper.'

'Go and cook; I'll stay here with my bow and arrow in case they come. Do you think she will die – I mean Obieke's mother?'

'I don't know, my son. May she not die for it would be terrible for us. Anyway, she won't. You did well to shoot her in the leg instead of the stomach.'

She went into the house. Having replenished the fire, she lit a fibre candle. She asked him:

'What will I cook for you?'

'Anything you like.'

'I bought some sliced cassava in the market. Can you manage it for supper?'

'Where is it?'

From the basket she took out the green packet. He came in. She gave it to him. 'Eat this and drink some water,' she said. 'It will keep you going till morning.'

She began to unpack the basket.

'The market was good today,' she announced joyously. 'I sold practically everything I took there.'

'And you said in the afternoon that I started you off badly!'

'You didn't, my son.'

She took out a raffia bag and spilled its contents noiselessly on the floor. They were cowrie shells. She counted them, in units of five heads, one head being six shells. They totalled up to fifty heads and five. Smiling, she put back the shells in the bag, after which he put the bag aside.

Next, she untied the cloth girdle round her waist. This was

the tube-like type, with one end sealed, which also served as a purse. She ran the girdle between her thumb and forefinger, from the closed end to the open, until the shiny coins dropped into her palm. They were three, all pennies, each of which was equivalent to thirty heads of cowrie shells. She must handle them gently, she told herself, lest they jingle and invite thieves. The trouble with metal money was that if you lost just one piece you lost a lot!

She took both the pennies and the bag of cowrie shells into the inner room. There she uncovered a hole under her bed and brought out a small packet done with the hard and opaque skin of palm-frond stalk. She opened the packet and counted. They were still twenty in number, all pennies. She put in the three new ones, tied the packet again and put it back into the hole. To divert attention from this spot, Chiaku left the raffia bag conspicuous at the opposite end of the room.

Back in the parlour she sat on a dwarf stool near the outer fringe of the floor, facing the fireplace. She stared thoughtfully at the fish basket hanging over the fire. After some time she heaved a sigh and said:

'There's something I want to tell you, Nnanna.'

'Tell me,' he mumbled.

She paused. 'But for you they would have torn me to pieces this night.'

'Is that the thing you said you would tell me?' He emptied another fistful of cassava into his mouth.

'Did you know that Oji has been asking us to come and live in my father's land?'

'Oji who is in Nade?'

'Yes, the one that is my brother. He has offered to build us a house and to give us land as well as fruit trees to own.'

'I like Oji very much. He calls me his in-law.'

'Which you are, for you are my husband's father come back to life. What I want to tell you is that we should now accept the offer. We can't stay here again. We'll go away before Amanze and his wives fire guns at us. They were about to tear me to pieces this night. You are listening?'

'Yes.' His jaws continued to work.

'We must run away, my son. It will be worse for us now that you've stuck your arrow into Obidia's leg.'

He said nothing. She wondered in her mind what his feeling was about the sudden proposal to abandon the environment in which he was well-known for a new one. Then she added an inducement:

'I'm sure you know that Idimogu's house is quite near to Oji's. You will have your friend Ibe there with you always; you will no longer have to travel from here to Nade to meet him, nor he from there to here for you.'

'Shall I tell him tomorrow?'

'Where will you see him?'

'He's staying with Oboka for the night.'

'Oboka who is his father's sister?'

'Yes. He will go back to Nade tomorrow morning. He was with me when Adagu and Obieke were abusing you in the evening.'

'They did?'

'Yes.' He told the part of the story that was in his favour.

'Amanze and his wives have sworn that we must die, my son,' said she sadly. 'All that will soon be over. We'll move to Nade; we'll do so without delay.'

'When?'

'When?' she repeated, thinking aloud. 'Why wait at all? We shall leave very early in the morning – before the chickens come out from the pen. We can come back afterwards for our things. We had better sleep now so that we can get up in time.'

Chiaku slept very little that night. When the cock crowed for the second time she ran her hand under the bed till she had found the hole. She took out the packet, opened it and transferred all the coins into her girdle. Then she woke him up with some vigorous shaking. Ten minutes later, they were already on their way to Oji's house.

THREE

A few days after Chiaku had arrived, Oji invited all the umunna to his house. The umunna were male members of the extended family which began with Ojemba, four generations back. He offered them four full pots of palm-wine, to which they did justice. Then he disclosed the purpose of the invitation. A daughter of the family had now returned to live among them, he said. Chiaku had come home with her son and she needed a house of her own.

'Of course we will build one for her,' the oldest of them replied. 'Just show us the land . . .'

'That's good talk and requires no other reply than action,' said another.

'And of course the child is now part of us; he is entitled to all the rights of a son of the family,' another added.

'Custom says so,' they confirmed together.

Then Oji spoke again. 'As far as land is concerned, I'll show you that before you leave. Also I have a big mound of well-trodden red earth which I had intended for my compound walls. We can use that for the house.'

'Then you will all have done your part,' the old man said. 'We Ojemba's children love one another as very few families in Nade do. We will work for our sister. We will supply the mats and bamboo and the labour too.'

Four moons later the house was ready and Chiaku moved into it. Then the umuada, direct female descendants of Ojemba, sent word that they would come and open the new house. This was a way of telling her to be prepared to feast them and to expect some gift in return. Chiaku replied at once: she would only be too happy to receive her sisters.

Days passed. There was only one day left. She had got the cassava ready; so also the yams, the fish and meat. It only remained to prepare them for eating. Then Chiaku discovered that there was not going to be sufficient water, for the big pot was only half-full, which was quite serious. Unlike at

Umudiobia, it took several hours here to fetch a single pot. That was because only one small stream served the entire population. She decided to appeal to Nnanna to go for more.

'Please, my son, go and fetch more water. You know we have a lot of cooking to do tomorrow.'

He shook his head. 'I've already fetched two pots today.'

'I know,' she pleaded. 'The fact is that the water we have will not do. Nnadim, please go.' Nnadim means My Husband's Father.

He was the reincarnation of his paternal grandfather. That was why he was called the name Nnanna. Those who had known the grandfather would often remark that the boy was a perfect image of him; that this edition, fully developed, was going to be even more handsome than the first. The oval face was there; so also the straight nose, the long legs, the elegance and the athletic build – those features which were hallmarks of male beauty. Then, to crown it all, he had a ripe-pear-black complexion. 'The mother who bore this child has many in one,' a visitor, herself a mother, did once comment. Nnanna was only five months and some days old then. 'And the father too,' Okafo replied with humour. 'Of course he is my father come back to life. Look at his face first. Nna – a!' He hugged, once more, the healthy baby who wriggled and kicked and cried in his hands, and he improvised a tuneless lullaby: 'I know you are hungry. But you must cry no more. For your mother is coming. No, Father; cry no more.' He kissed the child. 'She's cooking for your son. Obinna, please cry no more . . .'

Exactly twenty days later, Okafo fell from a tree and died on the spot . . .

After a good interval of silence, Chiaku repeated: 'Nnadim, please go; I've nobody else to help me. Fetch one or two more pots for your son's wife.'

He sighed bad-manneredly. 'You worry too much,' said he. 'Let me rest, I'll go in the evening.'

'Why not now? You could still go again in the evening.'

He sighed again.

'Are they in?' Someone called from the entrance door.

In his usual slow, leisurely strides, Oji walked across the front yard and entered the house. He sat down on a mud seat built on to the wall. There was a snuff-box in his left hand and an awkward smile on his broad face.

'This your house is small and cool, my sister,' said he, eyes on the roof. 'Our umunna did very good work for you.'

'True,' she acknowledged. 'It remains to build the compound walls.'

'I know. We'll see to that in the course of the year. There is sufficient earth-mud for it.'

'I'll be very happy when that is done.'

'You must invite the umunna for food one by one or in small groups – I hope you know. You've got to show them that you appreciate—'

'I'm not a child,' she interrupted. 'I have, in fact, invited some already. Oh, I don't remember whether I've told you!' she exclaimed regretfully.

'What?'

'That the umuada will be here tomorrow.'

'True? Your brother Oji knows nothing about it.'

'I thought you knew.'

'Who told me?'

'It isn't too late yet anyway. You can start now to prepare.'

'Prepare? Does one have to prepare before eating his sister's food? I shall come and sit comfortably among the guests.'

'I know you behave in a funny way at times,' said she, laughing. 'You could easily do that. Let's be serious now, you will please provide the wine. They will not be here tomorrow until after lunch time, so you still have time for that.'

He said: 'The way you women behave at times surprises Oji.'

'Have I not owned up to my guilt?'

He paused. 'Do you know it was only yesterday that somebody told me about it? What you've done is bad, my sister. However, I shall try to bring you three pots of wine.'

'Thanks, my brother.' Then she turned to Nnanna. 'Go now, his mother's hero; go and fetch water. You can call and see Ibe on your way, if you like. Perhaps he will decide to accompany you.'

Oji laughed enigmatically.

'What is it?' she asked, embarrassed.

'You said something about a hero.'

'Oh, that? I called him my hero. He is his mother's hero.'

16

'When did that one begin, if I may ask?'

'Of course he is. Nnadim is my hero.'

'Big name that kills a puppy! How many wars has your hero fought and how many heads did he take?'

'But there are no more wars these days,' she said with a smile. 'If there were, you would see him bring the heads home.'

'Never call him such big names again,' he objected seriously. 'They could drive him to his doom.' He said to Nnanna: 'Go and fetch water for your mother.'

'He will go,' she said. 'He is a good child, Nnadim is. You ask why I call him my hero? It seems you've forgotten what he did to them at Umudiobia the night before we came over to Nade.'

'He is a good marksman, I agree. Of course there's no asking whence he got the gift. Nwanolue, his father's father, was a good friend of our father and I knew him well. He and Father used to call each other Friend. Nwanolue was the man who routed Obizi warriors with his bow and arrows in one of the fiercest battles between that town and Umudiobia. He never shot and missed. Neither of his two sons got the gift. Only his grandson did.' He tapped at the snuff-box gently, wistfully, and opened it. He stirred the dark-brown dust with his right thumb and lifted a good pinch. 'But then, is that sufficient reason for calling him a hero or, as I overheard you once, a lion? Whom has he thrown in the town's wrestling square? Whom has he given a margin in mound-making? What brave deeds has your hero done apart perhaps from sticking an arrow into the leg of a wicked woman whom the gods probably don't want to be alive?' He smiled a stinted but genial smile, as a father, and emptied the snuff on his thumb nail right into the nostril. 'A-a-ah!' he exclaimed. 'It's meat itself, Nwada's snuff. There's none in this world to compare with it.'

'Wrestle?' said Nnanna, lifting the small water pot. 'I can throw anybody of my age you people produce in Nade. Gather them together and I'll drop them one by one.'

She grinned delightedly.

'You are lucky you are now with us,' Oji said.

'That has saved them then.'

'You must get ready to show your strength against Ozala.

17

But who can rely on limbs from Umudiobia? Can we rely on you?'

'All right, I will throw the boys hard during practices,' he said by way of a resolution. 'And I'll show them how to shoot and do everything.' Almost singing the words, he ran out, the pot on his head.

'He looks a boy of many parts,' Oji said to Chiaku. 'But you mustn't flatter him too much, my sister. A big name kills a puppy. By the way, is he the good wrestler he claims to be?'

'Even better,' she replied. 'They used to fear him when we were in Umudiobia.'

'Indeed! What else should I expect from you when every mother calls her child the best?'

'Not that; he's really good.'

'Umudiobia, ha-a-ah!' he sneered. 'That town of stiff joints! We used to throw them like lifeless bodies when we were young.'

She was amused. 'Did we ever see you wrestle, my brother?'

'He did not get the gift from Umudiobia – if he has it; he got it from Nade.'

'I accept whatever you say. Let Chiaku rest.'

They were both silent for some time.

'I saw Ezinne yesterday,' said he. 'I mean the one who leads umuada in song and dance. She asked me to inform you that they will make music when they come.'

'I'm at home,' she replied confidently. 'I'll satisfy them.'

'Did you say satisfy? Nobody ever satisfied umuada, my sister. Their stomachs are like the earth which is always hungry in spite of all it consumes. Just do your best for them.'

By lunch-time the following day the umuada started to arrive. By the onset of sunset they had formed a crowd over fifty in number. They sat in the open yard, on the dwarf stools they brought with them.

From inside the house, Chiaku came out with Nnanna to welcome them formally. A second later, Nnanna was lost in their midst, some fondling, all calling him their son.

'Have you greeted your mothers?' she asked him over the noise.

'He has!' they answered sharply, in his defence. Some begged her to leave him alone.

'Run across then and tell Oji that they have come.'

Nnanna was still trying to extricate himself from the tangle of hands when Oji came in. They greeted:

'Iweadinobi!'

'May it be well with you all,' Oji replied, waving at them confidently, like a popular politician. Iweadinobi was the most popular of his nicknames. It meant that there was no anger in his soul.

'Anger is of no use,' he added.

He had sat down. From the bag that hung down his left shoulder, he brought out kola nuts and alligator pepper. He touched these to his lips and held them out for the visitors to see. He said:

'I present kola. By custom kola is not to be shown to women before it is broken, but since there's no man here with me, I might as well let you see.'

They ordered him to break the kolanut without further speech.

'Fortunately for you, Nnanna is no longer here,' he went on. 'I should have been obliged to show it to him instead of to you.'

They made remarks about the amount of male in him and Nnanna put together.

When he had finished breaking the kola, he passed it to them to distribute, after which Chiaku brought out three big pots of wine. They drank one pot and as much of the second pot as was necessary to give each one two cups. Then the oldest among them clapped her hands and drew attention to herself. She said:

'Keep what is left of that wine and let's retire first in council. Much drinking should never precede any important talk.'

Most of them agreed. The rest asked for one more cup each, in reply to which they were advised to manage with their saliva.

Six of those who made up the committee of the umuada, one from each of the six homesteads in Ojemba's family, went out to confer. When they returned the old one spoke again:

'We've returned. We'll now announce our decision. Oji, it's good that you are here to hear our voice.

'Chiaku, your sisters have come to open your new house for

you. In doing that, we wish to welcome you and your son back to our father's bosom. What you must always bear in mind is that a child who has run into her father's lap should consider herself as safe.' She turned round and said: 'Is my voice not to your liking?'

'Get on with it,' they shouted their approval.

There was a certain one among them who by nature was incapable of disguising her feeling about most things. Her name was Onugo, but people called her Weaver Bird because of her pronouncedly pointed lips. She pecked:

'Amanze and his wives, may an iroko tree fall on their heads!'

They roared.

'Shut up, Weaver Bird!' someone said.

'You speak your mind like a mad one, my sister,' their speaker said, and then continued: 'Now that you are here, you will have to begin life afresh. We've therefore brought you some small help.'

She glanced sideways, thereby giving the signal. Somebody came forward, a raffia bag in hand.

'Take this and count.'

Silent, Chiaku received the bag. She spilled the contents before them, on a mat, and began to count. Some helped. They added up in the end. She announced:

'Twenty heads and ten in five places.'

'Twenty heads and ten in five places is what we give to you, our sister,' cried the speaker loud enough for all to hear.

'Thank you, thank you, my sisters,' Chiaku said, greatly moved, and began to put back the shells into the raffia bag.

'Thank you very very much,' Oji now spoke. 'Believe me, I could never have guessed that you women had so much in your possession. My sister Chiaku is very lucky indeed to have got all that from you. I want to leave you now, but before that, please give me some more wine to drink. Go well when you leave.'

'Fat one!' Weaver Bird pecked, playfully this time. 'He thinks we will leave here soon. That's how much he knows about receiving a sister.' She was about Oji's age and they used to be playmantes when they were small.

'Please forgive your brother,' Oji said. 'Forgive him and give

20

him two more cups of wine. Onugo, Weaver Bird, tell them to give me more wine.'

'No more for you,' ruled Weaver Bird with an ill-acting smile.

But before he left, Oji succeeded by jokes and flattery in getting three more cups of wine from them.

Night was fast setting in. Ezinne stood up. She clapped her hands a number of times and drew attention to herself. Then she announced.

'Umuada, remember, we'll stay here most of the night. We'll stay and sing for our sister.'

'We hear you well!' they chorused.

'For that we've brought our rattles and clappers,' she went on, almost singing. 'And we've brought our music pot and metal gong. It's part of our life, such dead-of-the-night clapping and singing. How much more when our sister needs to be sung for alive! We'll sing for her and call her name in our songs.'

'Your voice is a gong!' they applauded lustily. Some called: 'Beautiful one!' She was tallish and young, in her late twenties, slender and of a very fair complexion, with beautiful white teeth.

She picked up her clappers.

'We have fed and we have drunk,' she sang. 'We have got the strength to make good music. We must go on till it's dawn.'

'Gong!' they hailed. With that they bestirred themselves and began to pick up the instruments.

The clappers in her hands tapped for some seconds. 'Come now, make yours tap!' she called, still in song; and they yelled. She tapped again, giving the rhythm, and they joined in. The tempo was as yet slow.

She announced a song. They began to sing. With the song the tempo quickened and they put some vigour into the performance. The music pot came in, droning in monosyllables as the player fanned in air through the ear and compressed it at the misplaced mouth. Now and again the long metal gong would peal and Ezinne's voice, rising sweetly over the instruments, would ask Chiaku, their sister, and Nnanna, their son, to speak out if they found anything wanting in the performance.

They had performed for nearly half an hour without break. Then Ezinne said, weaving the improvisation perfectly into the rhythm of the music:

'It's now time to breathe. But before that, let's sing her a new kind of song. Listen, Chiaku, and hear it with your ears. Listen, Nnanna, it's meant for you too. And Iweadinobi, hear it from your house.'

They broke into another ecstatic yelling.

She sang the solo. It was the first of the three she had composed specifically for the occasion. Far and wide, even in parts of Umudiobia of ten villages and two, the hilarious chorus echoed in a shrill treble. It said:

> You've run into your father's lap
> And should consider yourself as safe.
> You still have a husband—
> He is Nnanna
> Who's also your son.

FOUR

He had just disposed of his supper with throat-choking speed. He lay at one corner of the parlour, on the bare floor, recuperating. Opposite him Chiaku sat on a small mat spread on the floor. She was still eating. She ate with ease and grace, her feet down and straight, the pot on her right. The moon was shining and the night had a cool and quiet splendour.

'You deposited the lumps inside your throat all at once,' she said in reproval. 'Now you pant like a lizard that has just dropped from a high wall.'

'I ate like a man,' he answered her with an air of superiority. 'See how you eat your own – like a snail crawling!'

She smiled indulgently. 'I can't understand why you should always rush over your meals. You throw everything in as if you stole the food and are afraid of being caught eating it.'

She lifted another lump. It was pounded cassava. She dipped it gracefully in the soup. Instead of conveying it to her mouth, she raised it over her head, and swung her hand round.

'Igwe, to you I pray!'

She threw out the lump of food.

It fell on a small but well-nourished plant near the entrance door. Since the day they moved into the house Chiaku had adopted this plant as the abode of her chi. With three throws or more every day she had now perfected her aims and could hit the spot even in thick darkness.

'Amanze and his wives, may they never meet good luck in this life!' she added. 'And may umuada live long!'

'You remind me, Mother,' Nnanna said. 'I saw Weaver Bird yesterday. She asked me to greet you; she also gave me a head of cowrie shells.'

'You thanked her?'

'I did.'

'She's a kind woman. You mustn't call her Weaver Bird again. That is only her nickname.'

'But that's what they called her that day.'

'You mean when they came here?'

'Yes.'

'They were only joking.'

She threw out another lump of food.

'Hu-u-uh!' he objected. 'You throw away too much food today.'

'Let such words never never come out of your lips again,' she countered. 'You have no respect for your mother's guardian spirit, have you? Perhaps you've joined that abominable group in town who go about saying things the ear should not hear. People call them church men but I call them lunatics.'

'I saw some of them yesterday.'

'You did?' Her countenance had turned grave. 'They are evil creatures. I am sorry for the mothers who bore them.'

He was no longer listening. His ears were on the sound of voices which had just started in parts of the neighbourhood. They were voices of children. Some sang, some croaked, while others cawed, all discordantly:

Come out, come out, one and all.
He that fails to come out at once,
Let four hundred goblins poison his supper
And let him die before it's dawn.

'Off I go!' he announced abruptly and rose.

'Where?' she demanded.

'To Ibe's father's house. That's where we meet for tonight's moonlight games.'

'You were out last night, weren't you? And you want to go again tonight.'

He ignored the question and made to leave. 'I'm late already,' he muttered and quickened his steps.

'Come back in time and don't let it be like last night,' she instructed.

He ran. 'Come out, come out, one and all. . . .' He had joined in the free song. The air was filled with voices and it seemed as if all the children in the neighbourhood were calling.

A few minutes later, he returned panting.

'What's wrong?' she asked.

'I forgot something,' he managed to say.

'What?'

He went to the corner of the room where he had been lying. He picked up something from there.

'You are going to eat groundnuts with coconut tonight?' asked Chiaku with a teasing smile.

He was listless. He ran out again.

By the time Nnanna arrived at the long and broad approach to Idimogu's compound a fairly large crowd had already gathered. There were boys as well as girls. They had also sorted themselves into four groups.

The smallest of the groups were the infants, as yet ten in number. They lay on their stomachs gazing at the sky, and took turns in reciting:

One star above, one grain of sand below;
Two stars above, two grains of sand below;
Three stars above, three grains of sand below . . .

Any that miscounted or hesitated for too long were dismissed with a boo and a volley of knocks on his head; then another would take over, starting all afresh. Those that counted successfully to the end were applauded. Another group, aged roughly between eight and twelve, were doing a mock warfare. They stood in two lines, facing each other, with about six feet between. One line sang threats and the other, responding, sang defiance. At the end of each such song, the latter would turn and take to flight and the former would pursue. Those caught before the finishing point stood out as war casualties. Then, continuing, the procedure would be reversed. And so on, until one of the sides would lose all its members and was consequently declared annihilated. A good distance away, and nearest to the entrance door, the third group performed. They were only girls, and they were aged anything from twelve to sixteen. They clapped and danced, in smaller groups of three or four. At the other extreme end, farthest from the girls, were the biggest of the boys, most of whom had, in varying degrees, begun to experience the tinglings of puberty. They were wrestling, in preparation for the season which was only two moons ahead. Now and then a small and mischievous male furiously pursued by a biggish female would crash into their midst. They would offer asylum to the fast-footed fugitive and pray the pursuer to come nearer a bit. The latter, sensing that it was one of the boys that had sent the small one to harass her, would return a deadly curse for the invitation and go back to her group. In spite of such harassments, everybody enjoyed the games. They sang and clapped and shouted, and for hours on end the noises rang with a happy dissonance over a wide area. And the moon poured its light.

It was well after sleeping time – even for the slow and unpunctual housewife. Parts of the approach were now littered with bodies of the younger ones whom sleep had eliminated from the games. The big boys broke the coconuts they had brought to the games, and separated the white lining from the hard brown shell. Then, slowly and with a conspiratorial silence, they moved towards the big girls and invaded them, without much opposition. Soon they were nearly all paired, one boy one girl, each avoiding a close relation. The boys gave coconuts to the girls; the girls gave groundnuts to the boys.

After the refreshment they all stood up and formed a circle, linking their hands.

They sang. At the same time they ran round and round. At the end of each song, which took two minutes or less, they would halt abruptly. Dazed and breathless, a good many of the girls would drop down on the ground. Then, with excessive zeal, their gallant partners would begin to lift them up; some took the opportunity to pinch the girls' muscles, after which they would run away, laughing. Those of the girls who attempted to pursue soon discovered that it was exactly what the rascals wanted; they therefore turned back, cursing. Hands joined again, they would begin another song and another rotation. And the moon poured steadily, indulgently. So bright were the rays this night that, as the saying goes in the area, they went piercing right into the centre of the earth.

The cock crowed for the first time. The moon had ceased to shine and a heavy darkness filled the universe.

'Nnanna!' Chiaku called. She rose from her bed. She called again; then again. Bending down, she ran her hands over the section of the floor where he was supposed to lie.

She moved to the direction of the door and groped until she had touched it. She opened it gently and went out to the parlour. An all-night fire smouldered at the fireplace. She kindled it, lit a fibre candle. Then she returned to the room to satisfy herself.

He was not there!

Chiaku went out to the parlour again. The candle was burning in her hand. She stood motionless and stared thoughtfully. She would go and see Oji, she resolved; she must go at once.

Ten minutes later she was knocking at the entrance door of Oji's compound.

'Who's that?'

Not until he had asked again did she answer.

'Who do you say you are?' he demanded aggressively.

'It's Chiaku.'

'Which Chiaku?' He began to come out.

'Your own.'

'Hoa-a-ah!' Oji cried hoarsely, to the very limit of his voice. 'Let any evil creatures that lurk take to immediate flight!' He

26

stretched and groaned and his teeth creaked. 'Tfia!' he spat, at evil creatures, both far and near.

'Is anything wrong?' he now asked.

'Open the door first.'

He opened. She stepped in.

'Is Nnanna here?'

In the wavering light of the fibre candle he regarded her in silent amazement.

'He is not in the house and I don't know where he is,' she clarified.

He yawned hollowly and began to scratch his forearms. As soon as his mouth was free, he asked:

'Is he reported missing?'

'He went out for moonlight games at Idimogu's house and has not returned.'

He heaved a sigh. 'Is that all? Is that why you should leave your house at this hour when spirits roam the earth?'

She was quite hurt by his attitude to the whole thing. She asked him: 'That's not sufficient cause for anxiety?'

'He isn't here anyway,' he said.

'Then I must go and look for him.'

He gave out a snort.

'Go back to your house, Chiaku, if you are wise.'

'I'm not wise.' She paused. 'You want me to go home and sleep when the child is missing,' she grumbled. 'I don't know when you will learn to take things seriously.'

Oji compelled himself to laugh. 'Who says he is missing? This is Nade where life is very safe. We are not Amako, or Ukani, or Ossa on a hill where the old chew the liver of their young.'

'Is that all you are prepared to tell me?'

'Something more. You carry that boy too much to heart. Do you think it's you who guards him? Don't forget that his chi goes about with him always. What is it our father used to say? – "anything that breathes is, by and large, an uncertain possession and one mustn't put one's heart too much in it".'

'You'll come with me?' she asked.

'Go where with you? So I have been bleating all this time?'

'I'll go alone then.' She turned and made to leave.

'Where do you want to go?'

'To all the neighbourhood.'

He laughed again: 'Try Idimogu's house first if you must go. He may be there with his friend.' He moved forward. 'All right, let's go – I've no choice but to follow you.'

Idimogu was an early riser, which habit he had cultivated out of necessity. A renowned wine-tapper, he would start the morning round before the palm of the hand was visible, and by breakfast time he would have the wine mixed with water, ready for sale or consumption. Oji was not surprised therefore when Idimogu answered at the second knock on the entrance door.

'Husband of the Tapping Knife!' he called.

'Who's that?'

'It's Oji.'

'Iweadinobi?'

'May it be well with you.'

'Anything wrong?'

'I'm afraid.'

'What happened?'

'My sister, Chiaku, is as good as dead.'

'Don't say!'

'Is her son Nnanna here?'

'Speak gently.' His voice had a funereal quality. 'This is night.'

'Is he here?' Oji repeated without much change in tone.

'Possibly. Yes, he is. He came in with Ibe before the moon sank.'

'You saw him?'

'Certainly. Shall I call him?'

'Please do, but open the door first. My sister Chiaku may yet survive.'

The door creaked.

Presently Chiaku stood face to face with Nnanna. The long fibre candle still burned in her left hand. There was a heavy silence. A big moth, white and furry, hovered over the flame. She caught it gently and threw it away.

'I now begin to recover my breath,' she said.

'What's all this, Oji?' Idimogu asked.

'Yes, she was as good as dead until she heard that her son is here,' Oji tried to explain. 'She is completely revived now. You

28

can't imagine what she was like when she came to see me.' He said to her: 'Your son is here; I'm going back.'

The moth returned. Launching a furious attack on the flame, it flapped its wings with conquering vigour. Chiaku caught it again. This time, she imprisoned it in her fist, taking care not to crush it.

'Don't blame your sister,' she apologized. 'This villain of a son didn't tell me that he was not going to return after the games. It's not that I didn't want him to stay with his friend; I only wanted to satisfy myself that he was alive.'

'Why didn't you tell her?' Idimogu asked the boys.

Neither Ibe nor Nnanna said a word in reply. They just looked on. It seemed they were more surprised than afraid.

'Let's go now,' said Oji to Chiaku. 'He can return later at dawn. Or would you like to carry him back in your mouth?'

'Or to wear him on her neck?' added Idimogu humorously.

They dispersed.

Back in the house Chiaku put the moth down on the floor and covered it with a small basket. She would remove the basket at dawn. If she should find the insect still there she would know that it was an ordinary moth; but if it should disappear she would know that it was inhabited by some spirit. When she lifted the basket a few hours later, Chiaku came face to face with a third possibility: the insect was dead and its wings were withered.

She went out at once to consult a seer.

The seer saw. A malevolent spirit had come in the form of a moth, he pronounced, shaking the divining seeds apoplectically. The spirit was after her son. Nnanna's chi was wide awake; that was why the spirit was foiled. Having abandoned the moth's body, the evil spirit would never return. She should make a couple of sacrifices to the gods, and should begin as soon as possible.

She began that very day.

FIVE

'I warn you again, you worry too much about that boy,' Oji said. That was several days after. They were in the forehouse of his compound and he was shredding the bark of some bamboos with which to re-pad his climbing rope.

She said nothing.

'I told you that some time ago; let me say it again. Don't put your heart too much in him.'

'What you say is true,' she admitted; 'but you know . . .'

'Know what?' he interrupted her. 'That he is your only child, is it?'

'Yes.'

'And so what? Are you the only woman in this world who had only one child? There are scores of others in Nade alone who have none at all. Tell me something else, please.'

She looked on meditatively.

'And by the way, he is old enough now to know how to climb a small palm-tree and how to tap. Those are things he could have learnt at Umudiobia but his uncle would not teach him.'

'Teach him? Would Amanze even ask him to carry a bag for him – for a single day?'

'Oh, that's the favourite son's privilege, isn't it – I mean carrying the bag for the father? You were expecting too much if you expected Amanze to let Nnanna carry for him when he has his own son.'

'Nobody carries for that wicked man,' said she passionately. 'He would not even ask his own child; he carries it himself everywhere he goes. You need to see him passing, with the dirty bag hanging down from his left shoulder and a bent stick in his right hand. He looks like a big vulture.'

Oji broke into laughter. 'You exaggerate, my sister,' he said. 'Certainly Amanze does not resemble a vulture. Yours is an enemy's mouth out of which comes nothing sweet.'

30

'Let it be. The fact still remains that Amanze wouldn't let even his own son carry the bag for him.'

'That's quite surprising. The child who carries an elder's bag has a very good chance of being a wise man in his life. He follows his father to meetings and places, and listens to the wise words the elders speak. The result is that he knows at an early age those idioms and proverbs with which we fool the foolish and baffle the stranger, and also the customs of the land. All that Amanze denies even to his own son!'

'I've told you he is a wicked man,' she said emphatically and with rising bitterness. 'He knows only how to lick his wives' feet.'

He reverted to the subject of her son: 'I shall soon make Nnanna a climbing rope and teach him how to step up a palm-tree.'

'Thank you, my brother.'

'We should also begin to consider getting him initiated into masquerade cult.'

She beamed. 'Our minds work alike, do you know. I've been thinking about that for some time now.'

He growled promptingly.

'And more or less, I've been preparing.'

'Have you?' he asked.

'I mean that I've been saving against that.'

'I see. I don't know how much you have saved, but I guess you'll have to save a lot more. There are other things ahead for him. Marriage, for example. You know very well that your brother is far from being a wealthy man and Amanze, who should really see to everything, will not help.'

'Please don't mention that man's name when we are discussing seriously.'

'I'm glad however you are yourself: you are strong and industrious and can face most of it alone.'

'How much do you think the initiation will cost?'

'Not very much really, in terms of money. You will have to buy most of the cassava though, as you've not planted much – certainly we've nothing that can approach the required anthill.' He was referring to the mound of pounded cassava, proverbially as tall as the initiate, which was demanded at the initiation. 'And of course you'll have to put something substantial in the soup before they can touch the food. Anyway, I'm sure you can do it.'

'I'll try. And the umuada will help.'

'Probably. But nobody can help your son when the cane begins to eat his flesh. Since he is strong and brave, they will beat him hard to know what stuff he is made of. If he cries or tries to escape they will refuse to show him the masquerade leaf.'

'I'm sure he will not flinch.'

'Boys as strong as he is are known to have flinched, my sister. Let's hope he will be able to go through it, for nobody will show the leaf to a boy who under duress would squeal the secret of the spirit world.'

'I follow you.'

'There's one thing Nnanna could do to help himself, though.'

'Tell me.'

'Let him try to impress them before the time. Let him wrestle as much as possible in the season, for example. If he does well and wins their love for himself I'm sure they will handle him leniently when he comes before them.'

'We should have no fear then, for he wrestles very well.'

'Let's watch first. Perhaps we'll be able to decide when to fix his initiation after this wrestling season.'

'That's all right. There's no hurry yet. After all, he is still a child.'

'How old?' he asked with an accusing smile.

'Hardly ten years and two,' said she offhand. 'He was born the year his father died, remember.'

'And that is ten years and two ago? Of course every mother believes her son was born yesterday.' He paused. 'If you don't know, it's almost fifteen years since Okafo died.'

Harvest was over and the wrestling season had begun. This was the time Nade proved its worth. For, though a comparatively small town, it boasted the foremost wrestlers in the wrestling zone which comprised ten towns or more.

Five years back, Akaka of Nade, nicknamed the inimitable, dropped Udenka Ogbajiokpukpu of Ozala. Udenka was the best wrestler Ozala had produced, at least within living

32

memory. His grips were terrific, so much that they won him the nickname Ogbajiokpukpu which means 'breaker of bones'. Yet Akaka brought him down in the square.

After that victory, Nade remained the undisputed champion among the towns that come to the square. Only once, three years back, did somebody try to upset the record.

Dimgba was the man's name. He was a tall and lanky, but very cunning, wrestler from Ujiji. He threw everybody that challenged him, until Anya of Nade, the artful gripper, came in to save the situation. Anya brought him down with a trick of dodge-and-pounce that was new in the area.

In the current season, an unfancied upstart from Nade had already eliminated Nwokeukwu, the best that the other side seemed to have.

All those were bouts in the top grade, the ones that really determined which town and which side was supreme. The victories were sufficient to establish Nade's supremacy. And yet, even in the lower grades, the wrestlers invariably won more than they lost.

There was one grade however in which for the past two seasons Nade wrestlers had lost nearly all their bouts. This was the lower-medium. In this grade wrestled boys aged approximately fourteen or fifteen. The gap was a sad one, the fans would comment; for a gap of the present was a gap of the future. If now they had no champion or promising lad in that grade, how could they reasonably hope to have one in the top grade when the present lower-medium would become the seniors – and that in a few years' time? It was necessary to beat Ozala and its side in this grade too, to find someone who could throw Iko of Ozala, that arrogant but talented performer who had so far thrown the best from Nade's side.

The time was well after supper. The moon shone in full tropical brightness bathing the earth below with its cool and pure splendour. Tomtom beats, fast and stimulating, echoed from different parts of the town. 'Remember, remember, all and sundry, tomorrow will be a day of muscles,' rolled out the tomtoms from time to time by way of a refrain. It was going to be a wrestling day – the fourth in the season. The last one was four days before.

It dawned early and bright, the light of the departing moon

merging into that of the rising sun. The townsmen, both old and young, hurried over the morning chores and by midday they had started to move towards the square. Soon the square was crowded. Yet more and more people continued to arrive. Many came from outside Nade – from Ekulu, Ujiji, Ozala, Umudiobia, Uzi, Achala, Ikpeze, Afala. Some even came from Obizi. For years now both fans and wrestlers from Obizi had been banned from the square. That was because their champion had employed a charm to topple his opponent. Obizi had just expiated the offence and were allowed to return as from that day.

The crowd formed themselves into a circle, large but as yet not thick, enclosing a space that was wide enough for the bouts. On one side, forming roughly one half of the circle, were Nade (the host and leader of that side), Ekulu, Uzi and two more towns from the north. On the other side were Ozala (her side's leader), Umudiobia, and towns from the south. The drummers of each side sat in their privileged positions in front. They were already drumming, relating in the cryptic language of hollow tomtoms the exploits of their champions, past and present, dead and living. Even amidst the general noise and bustle, it was possible to hear clearly the steady volley of beats, for these drummers, all experts and themselves retired wrestlers, had now, as the saying went in the land, lost their heads to the thing. They hit with extraordinary vigour, whipping out torrents of rhythm.

The early stage of the match was ordinarily interesting. This boy from this side threw that one from the other side and won prolonged applause instead of the more glorious ride on the shoulders which was reserved for bigger ones. Steadily the age of the wrestlers rose. Then it was time for the lower-medium.

There had been only three bouts in this grade when Iko of Ozala charged into the centre. There was a savage look on his face. The lesser ones there quietly withdrew, each to his side, leaving the entire space to him alone. He squatted for a few moments, stood up, looked right and left. He shook himself, then stamped his right foot forcefully on the dusty ground.

Ozala and its side roared with applause. 'Who will challenge and be crushed?' boasted the biggest tomtom in the set of five. 'Nade, what answer have you for this . . .?'

One boy came out and challenged. Soon after they had engaged, Iko lifted him and dropped him mercilessly on the ground. Grinning in mischief, he held the boy pinned on the ground. The tomtom droned in his praise. It jeered at Nade, calling the men all sorts of names.

Iko released the boy, who now sprang up and ran hurriedly into his side of the crowd. Then he jerked himself convulsively and stamped his right foot on the ground. His left arm crossed over his chest, he hit the crook with his right palm, giving out an explosive sound. After that he started to run round, close to the crowd. As he did so he clashed his right upper arm against his ribs. If he had completed a circle, he would have withdrawn as the undisputed champion among his grade for the day – just as before. But he did not. As he was about to pass Nade's half of the circle, a boy slightly younger in age but considerably taller, dashed into the open space just in time to confront him. It was not clear whether this boy had been squeezed out by the squirming crowd, or whether he wanted to challenge. They all watched with heightened interest.

Iko halted. He regarded the boy murderously. He squatted. The boy knelt down and waited. And then, a woman ran in amidst shouts of abuse and reprimand. She went straight to the boy and exhorted:

'Go on, Nnadim; wrestle with him. I'm sure you will throw him.'

Iko heard her. He was piqued at the suggestion that he could be thrown, more so by such an unknown thing. He flung out his left hand with contemptuous indifference and showed the palm.

Nnanna stretched out his own hand.

Nnanna was nimble and elusive, Iko short and thickset. The latter, an expert among his grade in the much-dreaded feint-rush-grip-and-throw, feinted and rushed with confidence, as if his was the right to win. Nnanna dodged. And from where she stood Chiaku called on the child (born only yesterday) to try hard (against the ancient fellow that wrestled with only infants). Oji, standing fairly close to his sister, kept on urging: 'Don't allow!' Ibe, a good distance away from both, ducked instinctively now and again and kicked with his leg up and down, right and left, so much that he nearly got into some serious trouble with those near him. Sometimes Ibe would bite his fingers; sometimes, when he saw Iko making one of his unnerving charges, his heart would skip a beat. Very few people indeed thought that Nnanna had any chance as he swayed and eluded his opponent and jumped from side to side. But while he was dodging he was watching for the least opening for a your-upper-arms-under-his-armpits.

With a reckless over-confidence Iko stretched out both hands as if for a hearty embrace, meaning to draw the opponent. In a twinkle, Nnanna's upper arms went into the exposed armpits. Nnanna followed on, allowing Iko not a moment to brave himself and settle down to the pressure, or to lock the attacking arms. On and on Nnanna pushed, and balanced himself more and more. Then he levered with his left hip. Nade and the allies were yet starting an anticipatory applause when he brought down Iko of Ozala convincingly on the dusty ground.

Chiaku and Ibe dashed off almost simultaneously. Like joint-owners they reached Nnanna before anyone else. Oji, unathletic today as ever, managed to move a few paces before the crowd burst in, cutting off his access to the victor. A few moments later, the crowd had formed into a procession, with Nnanna riding in front on many shoulders, including Ibe's. The procession went round and round, singing, cheering, boasting. They jeered at Ozala and Umudiobia in particular, at that side in general. They called their men women, and their women mothers of weaklings. Chiaku yelled after them pointing skyward. The drummers, still in their places, drummed and sweated and smiled, once more losing their heads to the thing. It took more than a quarter of an hour before the pandemonium ceased and the match continued.

SIX

Night had fallen when Nnanna returned that day. He was accompanied by a group of boys. They were friends and admirers, twelve in number. Welcoming them, Chiaku said:

'You have led him home like a hero.'

'We thought we should,' Ibe replied. 'He disgraced Ozala today.'

'Sit down and wait; let me cook some food for you. I hope your mothers will not be angry with you when you get home.'

While she cooked they sat in the open front yard and conversed. They talked about Nnanna's style; then about Iko's.

'He has no art at all,' said the one who was thrown. 'He grips like a beast, that short old man.'

'Is that why he dropped you the way he did?' someone asked.

'Like a bag of sand!' another added.

He answered them: 'In my own case I came out to try. Apart from Nnanna, not one of you had the courage. There are even one or two here who have never entered the wrestling space.'

'Whom have you in mind?' another asked, eyes on Ibe. They joined:

'Ibe, when will you begin to wrestle?'

'He is all head and commonsense, no brawn.'

'He has the sense of a grandfather . . .'

'What about Machie who is all skull and nothing else?' Ibe asked good-humouredly.

'Close your mouth!' Machie protested at once. He was a big-headed, lean boy of a cheerless disposition.

'No, he has got something else besides a head,' threw in another. Then:

'I know what is is.'

'The bunch, isn't it?'

'That's true. Machie, I'm sure the load is too much for you.'

'He can't run.'

'How could he with such a weight down at his waist?'

'That's why he's always sick . . .'

Lower and lower they descended, until Chiaku was forced to shout from inside the house:

'Will you shut up! You don't feel too shy to say such things?'

'Leave the fools!' said Machie bitterly.

'That's enough!'

One of them sniggered.

He was a playful and even-tempered boy who often carried his sense of humour to comic extremes. His name was Okaka. They fell on him:

'Head like a mallet.'

'Don't mind him. He is happy because his father has found him a wife.'

'Okaka, is that true or not?'

'No, she is one of his father's wives.'

'So his father is making her over to him?'

Smiling pleasantly, Okaka called all of them mad fellows. But they continued:

'Can't that woman be your mother, Okaka?'

'It was he who demanded that one in particular . . .'

She had finished cooking. She brought the food in a clay pot. She put it down before them.

'There's nothing I shall not hear from you children,' said she, stirring them. 'So you covet Okaka's good fortune?'

They said several things in reply. But she did not listen. She left them and hurried back into the house, smiling.

A few minutes later, the pot was empty.

'Let's all go out together one day to do some shooting,' Nnanna proposed.

One after another they welcomed the suggestion.

'When?'

'Let it be on the day after next wrestling match. That will leave us sufficient time to prepare our arrows.'

'Won't it be a market day?' Ibe reminded them.

'True. The day after that then,' another boy amended.

They decided to assemble in Nnanna's house. They would be there immediately after lunch. Each should bring a good quantity of arrows, for arrows would be the stake.

They all came in time on that day. For the preliminary round, they agreed to stake with four arrows each. Then they divided themselves up into twos. Each pair went and fetched a banana leaf. They tore off the blades, leaving the midrib.

There was an open space, a disused square, about three hundred yards behind Oji's compound. To this space the boys went carrying their bows and arrows and the midribs. As soon as they got there they began to prepare for the preliminary round, simultaneously. First, each one of them took out four arrows from his bundle; and each pair put their eight arrows together. Then, at the centre of the space, they drew a small circle. From a different point on the circumference of this circle, each pair took twenty paces outward, so that in the end they made six big arcs of the area. At the point where the foot landed for the twentieth pace, they collected a small heap of sand. Finally, they stood the banana leaf midrib erect on the heap of sand.

Then from the small circle the contestants aimed. They shot one after the other. The first in each pair to hit the target for the third time qualified for the semi-final and also won the eight arrows staked. Ibe was out on this round but he recovered all his arrows in the end, having contrived to be matched against Nnanna. Okaka was eliminated too. They told him it was one of the many things one should expect for taking over a father's wife while the father was yet alive.

For the semi-final they lengthened the shooting distance and staked with two arrows each.

Then came the final. There were three contestants. They lengthened the distance further still.

'What is the stake?' asked one of the three.

'Husband of the Bow,' Nnanna proposed.

'I accept,' the third said.

They stood the target erect on a heap of sand and returned to the shooting circle. The rest ranged round them wistfully.

The first missed. Nnanna shot next. He missed. The third missed too. Then they began the second attempt.

They all missed again.

'Let's make it the first to hit once only, not three times,' Nnanna suggested.

'Agreed.'

'Provided that if any two hit on the same round they will continue for a decider,' the third amended.

The first shot and missed. It was Nnanna's turn.

'Iko's bane!' Ibe eulogized.

'Hu-u-uh!' he snorted in acknowledgement.

'Make it now.'

'Of course I will.' Again, he studied his bow and the arrow that was set on it. 'What can these two boys do with such shaky hands as they have? How dare you compete with Nnanna?'

'Go on please,' demanded the other two impatiently.

'The hand that took a bird in flight!' Ibe hailed again.

'I am!'

'Take this one.'

'I will.' He tensed. He inclined forward slightly. Like his hands, his eyes were steady and in perfect alignment with the sharp point of the arrow and the target. Then he pulled – slowly . . . harder . . . harder.

Twang!

They roared.

'Husband of the Bow!' Ibe declared.

'Not yet; Ejike has not shot,' said Nnanna sarcastically.

Ejike took his turn and missed by a wide margin.

Then they all cheered and greeted Nnanna as Husband of the Bow. He raised both his hands and hopped up in triumph a number of times. After that, he shook hands with them one by one and acknowledged the praises. He knew from the start that he was going to win, he boasted. Would Ejike like to continue trying until the following day? His were special hands, if they had not known that before. Let nobody attempt to compete with him again . . .

They were all amused – even Ejike himself. Some told him he was just lucky. Okaka suggested he should be called Husband of the Mouth as well as of the Bow.

'Does anybody know why Machie did not come?' one of them asked.

'Yes, I know,' Ibe answered. 'So you've not heard?'

'What?' asked they with a sudden inquisitiveness.

'Machie has joined.'

'Joined whom?'

'The church. His father's brother who is a member, took him to the place yesterday.'

They exclaimed.

'Can't we force him to stop?'

'We can't,' Ibe answered.

'Why not?'

Nnanna took over: 'How can you? Unless you want them to come and plunder your father's compound.'

'Plunder your own *father's* compound!' retorted the boy offensively.

'Your father!' Nnanna pointed pugnaciously.

'Your father!' the boy advanced, his fists ready. 'It was you who called my father first, you dead body.'

Nnanna dropped his bow and arrows at once and stood well-balanced to deliver a blow. 'I say your father!' He shot his hand to within a few inches of the boy's face.

The others intervened and separated the two before the clenched fists could go into more positive action.

SEVEN

'I've come to remind you,' she said.

'About?' Oji asked.

'Nnanna.'

'What about him?'

They were in the open frontyard of his house and he was sharpening a matchet on a big whetting stone. The farming season was just starting. This was the time when, as the saying went, the whetting stone groaned loudest and pined most.

'His initiation into masquerade cult.'

'Oh, that? I've not forgotten.'

'Isn't it time yet?'

'You say?' He stopped abruptly.

'I suggest it's time now.'

'How do you know? Let's wait a little more.'

'For how long, please?' She was disappointed.

'Next harvest season or so. Let's give him more time to prove himself. Give him work to do. You really did very little for him at Umudiobia, as far as farming is concerned. But of course it isn't your fault, my sister.'

'What could I have done for him when I hadn't even the ground on which to stand?'

'I know.' The knife continued to grate. 'You should get him to work hard. If he refuses we can threaten to put off his initiation indefinitely.'

She said: 'Your point is quite clear to me, but we mustn't delay it for too long.'

'Delay? Have all those boys with whom he moves been initiated?' asked he. 'Left to you you would get him initiated tomorrow morning. Let him work for you this season and after that we shall see about his initiation.'

'Talking about work, you have not shown me the land yet.'

'I thought you weren't going to farm this year – like last year.'

'I couldn't have done much last year when we were still settling in. As for this year, surely it isn't late yet.'

'It almost is. The first heavy rains which warn the late starter, have fallen. However, I can still give you land. It's there waiting for you.'

'When can I have it?'

'Come back tomorrow morning and I'll show you the place,' he said. 'I am busy now.'

The next morning Oji took her to the thick and mature bush behind her house. Pointing, he said:

'This land, with all the fruit trees thereon, belongs to you, my sister. It hasn't been touched for years. And it extends as far as to that tall iroko tree, and on the other side to the cotton tree.'

She surveyed the area with her eyes. 'That will do,' said she with a grateful smile.

'Without doubt. I'm sure it can take four hundred mounds of yam in four hundred places.' He chuckled. 'And believe me, it has been waiting for you since our father died.'

She nodded cynically, yet pleasantly. 'I know. It can take as many mounds as there are stars in the sky. And it's been waiting for Chiaku since Nade began.'

'Yes, it knew that its daughter would one day return to it, and so it turned my mind away from itself,' he went on. 'Get

42

part of it cleared at once and plant in the soil the yams you brought home from Umudiobia – the ones I planted for you last year. I'm sure you will reap tubers that are taller than Ofokansi.'

'Who is he?'

'Have you forgotten the half-wit who smiles at women?'

She laughed until her body shook and tears came to her eyes. 'Will you help me to clear the bush?' she requested.

'Help you?' Oji asked. 'Have I got the time? Don't forget that I am to work for myself and for my wife, and also for my in-laws. There won't be much left of your brother after.'

She clicked her tongue in disappointment but by no means rudely, while he regarded her with a persuasive smile. People said they blended like salt and oil, Oji and his sister Chiaku, in spite of the ten years between them. They had been like that from their childhood.

They were now returning to the house.

'What about your son?' he suggested. 'This is your good chance to get him to prove that he is your hero and husband and other things. Let him show that he deserves the expenses of his initiation. ' His voice rose. He spoke with some feeling. 'If you want the young to grow up into useful men, you must find them something to do most of the time. Have you heard about Idika's son? Machle is his name.'

'I was stunned, my brother,' said she elliptically. 'Anyway that boy never looked as if he was going to be something in life. You need to hear how wretched the other boys used to make him. Last time they came to my house, I thought he would hang on his way home.'

'Two days ago I saw some of them at midday. Do you know what they were doing?'

'Tell your sister.'

'They were hunting for squirrels when they were expected to be working for their parents. That's what we see in Nade these days? No wonder the evil gathering appeals to them. They go there to learn to be idle.'

'I agree with you entirely,' said she.

'Keep your son always usefully employed, please. You know what you could do?'

'Yes?'

'Get him to form a mutual-aid team with his friends. Let them work for each other's parents in turn.'

There was an interval of silence.

'That's a very good suggestion, my brother,' she acknowledged. It requires no reply other than action.'

'Act on it then.'

'I will, certainly. Very soon, too.'

That same day Chiaku asked Nnanna to bring his friends for a meal. She gave the date and time. She would cook something special for them, she said. They should all come, for there would be enough to satisfy everybody.

The eleven of them came on the appointed day, Nnanna making the twelfth. She served them mashed breadfruit mixed with maize. After that she brought two bowls of the porridge variation, to which they also did justice, eating with small shell-spoons. From the way they now spoke she sensed that they had come to that agreeable mood to which the menu usually reduced children. She came out to address them.

'Long legs and open mouths!'

They asked her to mention names.

'I'm glad you've left the evil thing that is called Machie. He is not good enough for your company.' She paused. 'I don't remember seeing you boys at farm work. You only know how to shoot and wrestle. I would like to watch you one day clearing the bush for your parents. The best thing is to form yourself into a team. Can you do that?'

It was one of the easiest things in this world, they confirmed.

'You work for one boy's mother, then for another's, and so on, until you've worked for everyone's mother. We used to do that when we were your age. Would you like to do it?'

They would, they replied. Already they were seeing visions of themselves eating meals, with something substantial in the soup, cooked by the mother for whom they would work.

'We will tell our mothers first,' Ibe said.

'That's very sensible indeed, my son,' she replied. 'Tell them immediately you get home. Tell them also that you will start with Nnanna's mother. If you let me know in time when exactly you intend to start, I shall arrange for something to put in the soup for you.'

A few days later they sent word that they would begin the work after the following market. Then, a day before the time, they assembled in her house in the evening. They were only nine now, including Nnanna. The remaining three sent excuses. The nine spent the whole evening sharpening their knives.

When it was night she served them supper.

Feed well, my sons,' said she, radiating motherliness. 'I want you to have the strength to work for your mother like stalwarts. But don't eat like the ten stupid Obizi men we hear about in story, who woke up at noon after a heavy supper the night before.'

They wondered what the ten men must have looked like on waking. Some went on to speculate on what it was that the men ate.

The meal was on the whole peaceful, even though one of them was forced to complain, in the interest of fair play, about Nnanna's speed; and another about the size of Okaka's lumps. Towards the end an important question arose. Who should divide the thing in the soup? The 'thing' was fish and meat, expensive food items to which children must refer in such vague language. It was believed that taking liberties with the actual names induced dishonest habit in young ones.

'Okaka, of course,' someone suggested. 'He is the youngest here, even though he is the only married one among us.'

They went off: 'Is she pregnant yet?' 'How is she?' 'When will the child arrive?' 'Okaka, you've gone far in life.' 'No wonder you've been looking so well of late.' 'Why don't you start thinking about a second wife?'

Okaka called them barking puppies and returned them to the subject in hand. 'Who said that I am the youngest here?' asked he.

The argument raged. Then they decided to refer to their hostess.

'Mother, tell us who here is the youngest.' Ibe spoke, shouting so that she could hear.

From the backyard Chiaku replied: 'Are you in doubt about who should share the thing in the soup?'

'Yes.'

'Well, you are nearly all the same age,' she said. 'I think, though, Okaka is a few moons younger. Nnanna was three moons old already when I went to see his mother newly delivered.'

Okaka submitted to the decision. He cut the meat and tore the fish into pieces, and began to divide. Presently he announced, licking his ten fingers:

'Ready now. Who takes first, who second?'

All of them, with the exception of Okaka, contested the first place in age. They consulted their hostess again.

'Each of you claims to be the oldest, I suppose,' said Chiaku. 'I shall decide that for a fee. Are you willing to pay?'

'What is it?' they asked.

'Not much, only I won't decide until you have paid. And you can't pay now; you will pay tomorrow.'

'I'll take my own share now,' somebody threatened.

'Touch it and see in what state you will find your lips!' Another: 'What did he say he would do?' Another: 'Long throat! You've never seen something in soup before, have you?'

Chiaku suggested: 'Why not close your eyes and stretch out your hands for whatever Okaka may give you? As for your age, I shall tell you when you have paid the fee.'

They accepted the suggestion.

'Mother, you haven't told us the fee,' Ibe reminded her shortly after.

'I know,' said she. 'You will pay it tomorrow and with your knives. He who clears more and better than the rest, for him will I decide.'

It was time to sleep. They lay in the parlour, on two large mats spread on the floor. They chattered and chattered, rambling from this to that.

'I saw a wonderful dance last time I went to Umueri with Father,' said Okaka over the noise. 'After watching it I said to myself: "We must learn this one".'

'How is it?' asked someone.

'It's simply wonderful,' said he. 'Why don't we learn it? We haven't learnt any yet.'

'Tell us how they dance it and stop bluffing!' several voices demanded.

He told them that it could not be described. They shouted at him impatiently. What did he go to Umueri to do by the way? Was it to look for a second wife?

'The dancers are of the age-grade above us,' he vouchsafed. 'They moved fast and the drummers hit hard. They were all dressed in red and black. Father says it is called Ukwueluani. Believe me, it is hard to describe.'

There was not much discussion before they agreed that they should learn the dance.

'Ibe has not said a word,' someone remarked. And truly, Ibe had been silent all this time.

'I say your head!' he answered sharply.

Another intervened, thereby saving the situation: 'Okaka, tell your father that we wish to learn the dance. You will be appointed the leader, since it's you who discovered it.'

They all objected. 'Okaka to lead whom?' they asked. 'How can he with his type of legs?' Okaka was noticeably bow-legged.

'It's going to be an imitation duck dance,' said Ibe dully yet effectively.

They roared with laughter while Okaka forged his own weapon.

They left for the bush as soon as dawn was complete. They had a short break at mid-morning for breakfast. By the time they returned finally the sun had begun to set. They had cleared the greater part of the bush, with the dense and thorny undergrowth in places.

Chiaku was certainly happy that they had done so much in a single day. But that was not her only concern; she had also observed their individual performances. From what she saw, and from the admission of the boys themselves, there was not the least doubt in her mind as to who had set the pace. On each of the three occasions she went out to see them, she had, with the surreptitious look of a mother, observed Nnanna and one other clearly ahead of the rest. She had seen the two tearing the thick green bush, thorns and creepers notwithstanding, at a rate she thought amazing for their age; she had watched them hook and slash with the strength and determination of adults. This evening Chiaku felt within her a sense of both success and triumph. In a happier environment here in Nade, reflected she, Nnanna's potentialities were becoming manifest. But she must not let him know her feeling: Oji had warned her against that.

During supper that night the boys raised the question of age again. Smiling, she told them:

'You all saw what happened. There was a tie. I shall be better able to decide for you when you return in a moon's time or so to make the mounds. That's actually what determines who is a man, not such a simple thing as clearing the bush.'

Perhaps, thought she within herself, in that mound-making too, the most strenuous of all farming activities, Nnanna would give most of them a good margin. He probably would. Wasn't he a gift to her? And many in one! Then Chiaku proceeded to build a mental picture of her son Nnanna in ten years' time. Tall, well-proportioned, handsome . . . a man of great skills and strength . . . a masquerader, wrestler, hunter, dancer . . . a successful farmer with twenty double rows of rich, rotund yams in his barn . . . the husband of two and father of many. In short, the best that any mother could expect in a son. At that time he should be in a position to return to Umudiobia. There, continuing the lineage, Nnanna would recover from Amanze all that had belonged to Okafo; he would build up the homestead and keep the ama – the approach to the homestead – open and broad, and in a good state . . . But should she not start now to think about having images of him? Yes, she should begin to look for a good girl who would produce his images, sweet restless things whom she could carry in her arms and lap, or hug to her breast, and who would grow up to call her Big Mother.

Continuing the reverie during her supper, she threw out a sizeable lump of food. It landed perfectly.

'Igwe, please accept,' she prayed silently. It was an offering to the god that ruled the universe for the welfare of her one and only son because of whom she suffered and struggled with undiminishing strength.

EIGHT

'There's something very important I've been meaning to discuss with you,' she said. 'Have you time for it now?'

'Time?' Oji asked. 'It depends on what you want to discuss. But whatever it is, please allow me to go and tap the palms first.'

'We can discuss it right away,' she insisted.

'No.' He shook his head. 'Wait till I return!'

'Isn't the shadow yet at the feet?'

'What is it about?'

'Should we pry when we are about to open the packet? Anyway it's about Nnanna.'

'Come to the obi then.'

Inside the obi, Oji put down the climbing rope and the tapping knife. He removed his snuff-box from the usual place on the rafter. He sat down, opened the box, emptied a liberal pinch into his nose. Instantaneously, his face contracted and he cried out painfully:

'Very very bad snuff! It stings the brain . . . Tfia to Onugo, the Weaver Bird!'

'You bought from her?' asked Chiaku sympathetically. 'I had thought Nwada was your permanent supplier.'

His head still battled with the acid sting. 'I had to buy from her because Nwada had none to sell,' he explained. 'Tfia to Long Beak!'

'Of course Onugo has never been a good hand at tobacco grinding,' Chiaku said. 'You probably bought from her because she is our relative. He who buys from his kin does not often make a good purchase.'

'The proverb is very true, my sister.' He pressed out teardrops from his eyes. 'Tell me now, what do you say is wrong with your son?'

'I only wanted to suggest that we begin to look for a girl for him,' said she reflectively.

He gazed impassively at the log of wood before him. After some time he said:

'Yesterday it was his initiation into masquerade cult. Today it is his marriage.'

Chiaku felt rather disconcerted. 'Do I err?' she asked with near-babyish frankness.

'Not at all.' He looked up, facing her. 'But tell me first, whose daughter have you in mind?' His legs began to shake.

'Who's talking about whose daughter already? I was only suggesting that we begin to look for a girl.'

He steadied his legs. His face brightened a bit. He said: 'You know, Chiaku, you often show the sense of a man. Especially when it comes to that boy.'

'Am I not both father and mother to him?' she asked in reply.

There was a pause. 'I agree with you,' Oji said. 'Your son has been developing very fast of late . . .' He went off, describing with realism the physical manifestations of adolescence which he had lately observed in Nnanna. 'But you must have had somebody in mind,' he concluded. 'Such thought usually comes when one has seen a possible girl. Tell me plainly, who is she?'

'Nobody yet, I should say,' she said hesitantly.

'Go on.'

She smiled guiltily. 'I seem to like Nwada's first daughter – now that your snuff has reminded me about her.'

'Nwada, from whom I usually buy my snuff?'

'Yes.'

He guffawed. 'And you said you had nobody in mind?'

She evaded: 'What do you feel about that one?'

He laughed again, in a mystifying manner, and said: 'Your ignorance is pardonable perhaps.'

'Ignorance of what?'

'The girl is our flesh and blood.'

'Is it close enough?'

'It is, my sister. Listen.' He reeled off with the genius of the people for remembering their genealogy: 'Nwada is Nkembu's daughter. Nkembu is Nwakama's son. Nwakama's mother was Nwego who was Ojemba's sister.'

Her eyes opened wider and her fingers snapped.

'And of course you know that Ojemba is our great-grand-father. Custom forbids that a man should marry his sister. You remember the recent scandal about Ugokwe and Enyinna?'

'Very well,' she said. The story still rankled. Ugokwe had become infatuated with Enyinna who was his third cousin, and before anybody knew what was happening they were already expecting a child. The whole town cried abomination. To keep off the evil spirit that must have put the idea into their two heads, people set up crossbars on two sideposts at the approach to the compounds and hung up the sacred Umune (New-bouldia) leaf there. Passers-by, seeing the leaf, would snap their fingers and exclaim: 'Let nobody allow the evil spirit to enter his compound!' In their moonlight games, on their way to the stream, or even while at work, children sang about the two, more especially about Enyinna. The soloist would call:

> Who'll sing me the story
> Of a certain girl and her brother?

The rest would answer:

> I know the girl
> And I know the boy
> Enyinna she is – that bad girl
> Who knows no shame at all!
> She now has behaved like a bird
> And flown to marry her blood
> Come now, all cry in horror—

Then they would shout to the limit of their voices:

> Enyinna yo-o-o-oh! Enyinna yoh!

'Well?' Oji said.

'I knew we were related to Nwada somehow, but I didn't know it was so direct.'

'It is. We can't marry her daughter.'

Neither of them spoke for some time. Then she asked:

'What about Odu's daughter? I mean Odu of Isieke village.'

'Do I know her?'

'Perhaps. Ego is her name. Her mother sells fish.'

'Could that be the one I know?' he wondered aloud.

'Maybe.' She described her further.

'Yes, I know her – quite well too.' He cleared his throat, teasingly. 'But didn't you say you had nobody in mind?'

No reply.

'She is from good parents – I'm sure about that. The family is obi, without doubt.' Obi, the small and unpretentious room-less forehouse in a compound, had always been exalted into a concept. A family was called obi if it possessed not just the physical house, but also a clean history and a reasonably hope-ful future. In addition, the founder must have been a free citizen and not a slave or one consecrated to a shrine.

'I think she will develop into a big woman – like her mother,' she said.

'She should fit your son. But then, we won't marry only her body; there are other things to consider. Is she strong, obedient and industrious? You must inquire extensively, my sister. He that goes into marriage without the necessary inquiries, let him be ready to have in his house a scoundrelly chatterbox. So our father used to say.'

There was a tap at the entrance door, followed by:

'Is Oji in?'

'Who's that?' Oji asked in reply.

'I, Idimogu.'

'Husband of the Tapping-knife?'

'Hu-u-uh!' Idimogu snorted.

'Come in.'

Idimogu's face was like an overcast sky.

'What's wrong?' Oji asked.

'Oh, Chiaku is here too!' he said mournfully. 'Oji, a big bullet has hit my head.'

'What happened?'

He sobbed and gnashed his teeth. 'A man should eat his sorrow in his heart; if not I should have been in tears.'

'What's wrong?' Oji repeated.

'It's Ibe, my son.'

'What happened to him?'

'He has joined them.'

'Whom?'

He gnashed his teeth again. 'Yes, Ibe has joined the evil gathering which the land abhors.'

52

'Say not!'

He was silent. Oji regarded him commiseratingly while Chiaku kept on exclaiming and pulling her fingers hysterically. Then he expanded:

'Nduru, my in-law, has taken him to the place.' Pause. Then he expanded:

'Nduru, my in-law, has taken him to the place.' Pause. (Nduru was one of the more popular mispronunciations of the name Andrew.) 'Nduru swore to me some time ago that he would not rest until he had taken my son Ibe.' Pause. 'He has done so now.'

'Hei-hei!' Chiaku cried and gazed eloquently at Oji, her hands folded across her chest. 'What will Chiaku not hear in this world!'

'Sit down, Idimogu, and have some snuff for your nerves,' Oji said. 'I wish I had something better.'

'I can't sit and can't snuff, Oji,' he declined. 'I've only come to find out if Nnanna too has joined.'

'Nnanna?' objected Chiaku with a frown. The suggestion that Nnanna could join hurt her severely. 'He can't,' she added, assuredly.

'I'm going,' said Idimogu, dolefully. 'Let me go and think it over at home. It's either Nduru or Idimogu in this world – both of us cannot live at the same time.'

'No such thing, Idimogu,' Oji warned. 'They will throw you into jail if you attempt anything. They may even cut off your head. You'd better go home for the moment. Go home and think like a man.'

He went away dreamily.

'A terrible thing for Idimogu,' Chiaku remarked.

'Not only for him, my sister,' replied Oji with much concealed meaning.

'Does he know – I mean Nnanna?'

'How can I tell?' He looked absent-minded.

'Do you think he does?'

'The youth know one another's secret. But perhaps he does not know this one.'

'I thought Ibe was a good boy. I never knew.' She shrugged.

'They often disappoint,' Oji replied. 'Especially when they come to this age.'

She exclaimed once more and snapped her fingers.

'Listen, Chiaku.' He spoke with unusual gravity. 'I've not told you this for a long time now. In fact, I've not mentioned it since you returned from Umudiobia.'

'What is it?'

He hesitated. 'Why not re-marry?'

She went into a dreadful fit – as dreadful as what he had experienced the year before, on that day when he invited her from Umudiobia and advised her to marry again. On that occasion she virtually ran away from the forehouse, swearing, shouting at him. His only offence then, as now, was that he advised his sister to accept a suitor and leave Nnanna to the care of his chi.

The atmosphere was tense. Her mouth opened and closed, without a single word. He said to her: 'Forgive your brother. He has committed a hideous crime.' Then Oji took up the rope and the knife. 'Let me go and tap the palms.' He left.

She was still speechless. She sprang up from her seat. She went out to the open frontyard. There she began to walk up and down, like one bereft of her senses. Her face was a heavy cloud. She was burning with anger.

'I'm going to Idimogu's house to warn him about Ibe!' she cried, to nobody in particular. 'If that villain comes to my house again I will grind his feet in a mortar.' She gasped. 'And I will cut off his lips with a sharp knife if I see him talking to Nnanna.'

'Don't go and add to their sorrow!' warned Oji who was now perched midway up a tree.

The voice sounded to her like a mocking echo.

NINE

When bald-headed Francis Osita, alias Ositason, arrived in Nade to start the church, hardly anybody took him seriously. The rulers merely left him at the mercy of the most prominent witch-doctors of the land. That was in the year 1919, or, in the language of the people, immediately after the great epidemic which shook its victims until the jaws knocked and the bones rattled.

Francis came from Ania which was also his home town. Ania was well-known as a distant land which lay along a big flowing body of water, the place from where new things were coming into the area. Hardly three months after his arrival, he got into very serious trouble.

It happened that he was strolling along the very broad path which bordered the church premises on the north. He met a short, swaggering masquerade accompanied by an equally short youth. They were coming from the opposite direction. The masquerade growled and ordered Francis to keep out of the way or face something horrible.

'Nonsense!' Francis answered. He kept steadily to the middle of the road. It seemed as if he was bent on a head-on collision with the spirit.

'Keep out of the way,' the masquerade ordered again.

'Do you know to whom you are talking?' he replied imperiously.

'To a big fool who doesn't value his life,' said the masquerade, after which it crowed like a big cock.

He was nettled. 'Hinterland fellow!' he said. 'How dare you speak to me like that?'

'That's for a spirit?' the attendant wondered aloud.

'For a masked idiot.' His hands went up to his hip in defiance.

Then before him the masquerade waved the small, black idol in its hand. After which, it ran away, the attendant following closely behind.

A few days later, Francis discovered big leprous patches all over his body. He left Nade before the story spread.

His successor was a man whom most of the natives called Ji Oji (Oji's Yam), which was a wilful mispronunciation of his actual name, George. George was of the type that went to any possible length, physically, with those who resisted conversion. One day he came out to the market square to preach. Soon after he had started, he proceeded to rant against pagans and idols, threatening them with one type of fire or the other. Some of his audience, answering, called him a lunatic orator; some just snapped their fingers in their horror at the things that were coming out of the lunatic's mouth. But none would disturb him, beyond such remarks, as he did the solo act, swaying his big frame and pitching his husky voice with concentration over the babble. He was a fairly old man, in spite of his youthful zeal and energy; and he had a prepossessing appearance which he owed in part to the colour of his skin, for he just managed to escape being an albino. George had been sold as a slave in his younger years, but providence, through his skin, later brought him to the notice of the priest at Ania. It was the priest who rescued him, took him on, and gave him that veneer of education that was considered sufficient to preach the word of God with.

He had spoken for nearly half an hour. He tried to summarize. Beaming his sharp small eyes at the audience and punching steadily at the air, he said:

'I tell you again, men and women of Nade, it's very foolish to say that spirits inhabit trees and bushes. It's even more foolish to talk about idols. Come and join the church, all of you, and stop those foolish things you do. Come and worship God. And when I say God I mean the only true one. Igwe which you people adore is nothing, and his shrine there' – he pointed northward – 'is only a hut over a mound of earth.'

The crowd roared at him. Some said: 'Go and touch it if it is nothing and see what will happen.' But the ones with a high sense of humour just remarked that Oji's yam was completely rotten.

There at the square with George were almost all his converts, as yet about twenty in number, some of whom were very enthusiastic about the thing. Take the two friends David and Dominic. Throughout Nade, these two men were better known as ex-slaves than as anything else. Slavery had been abolished, it was true; but that did not mean that a freed slave was now equal to a free-born. After all, who did not know which families were obi and which were not?

Over the years, David and Dominic had fretted under jibes of this nature. Then the church arrived and preached, among other things, equality of all human beings, great or small, man or woman, slave or free, before the Maker. Taking advantage

56

of the teaching, they rebelled against their status. They were the very first converts George made in the town.

Now, David and Dominic accepted the challenge thrown to their master. Unknown to him, they proceeded to Igwe's shrine which was about three hundred yards away. About twenty minutes later, a mournful cry arose from there. 'Igwe has been assaulted!' the voice said and added something ponderous about the sky coming down to meet the earth. It was Osuigwe's voice. Osuigwe was the head priest of the shrine.

Not until two days after was the extent of the damage done to the shrine made public. David and his friend had pulled down part of the hut and mercifully liberated all the livestock tethered there as offerings to the god. They had also thrown handfuls of sand on the dome-shaped earth-mound inside the hut. The mound, painted the azure colour of clear sky, was the god in substance.

Nade seldom acted in a hurry and they did not in this case. Full twenty-eight days passed. On the morning of the twenty-ninth, David and Dominic were both reported dead. The story went that each of them had died quietly, and in his own house. It was Igwe that did it. The god had deftly, in a smooth and dignified manner, removed their spirits from their bodies, people said. As for teacher George, his violently jealous wife soon came to the town's rescue. She hit his left eye with a big wooden spoon during a well-matched and fierce fight between the two. It all started when missus, a big scowl on her face, accused him of ogling the womenfolk while preaching in church. It ended with his having to leave Nade almost blind in one eye.

Joseph who came next was a young man, aged about thirty. He was quite cool-headed and calculating in his ways. Francis had offended the masquerade world and that had ruined him, he told himself. George had been too aggressive in his approach. He was going to move cautiously. Before any important step, he would first of all study the wind, like those dark-skinned and lanky adventurers whose dug-outs perilously plied the big river at Ania. He would make a special effort to win the young who in future would be fathers and mothers and the leaders of the town. For such young ones, and also for as many of the older ones as cared to attend, he would start a school.

Joseph's success was phenomenal. Within four months of his arrival, he had well over a hundred members in the church and there were forty in the school. Then Nade was seriously perturbed. Especially the rulers. What troubled them most was the new thing called school. The church was bad enough, they said for it taught what the ear should not hear. The school was even worse: it took away children from their parents every morning and taught them not to work in the homes – in addition to everything! Yet these were the young ones who would grow up one day to be fathers and mothers. If they were left like that, the whole land would certainly perish with famine; not only that, they would destroy, sooner or later, all the sacred and time-honoured things by which the community was sustained, and tread on the graveyards of such things. But Igwe was wide awake! Igwe would not allow that to happen. His wolf still moved on his bidding. It would one day roar and come down on that assembly of the unworthy, and strike all of them dead.

Indeed the rulers expected that the wolf, thunder, would take care of the situation, now that witch-doctors had failed. But the wolf did no such thing; rather, membership of the place kept on increasing. They were therefore compelled to meet again and think about some more positive action.

It took several days before they came to a decision. They agreed that there could be no question of using violence. Such an action would certainly invite a gruesome carnage from the Commissioner's soldiers at Ania. How could they allow the whole town to be shot down because of the lunacy of a few individuals? They should rather denounce the place openly, and forbid from going there everybody who called himself a native of Nade. That had not been done; they should do it now without any delay.

They took the decision in the morning. In the evening of that same day, they assembled again. From their skin bags they brought out their pocket-size idols. Then the oldest one among them prayed:

'Let the gods wipe out this thing that has come into the land in our time!'

'Ofo!' they chorused. Simultaneous with the word, they touched the object lightly on the ground.

'May the spirits of our fathers prevail!'

'Ofo!' The idols came down again.

'May custom prevail!'

'Ofo!'

The following morning, at that hour when the palm of the hand begins to get visible in the light of the waking sun, Ikolo boomed. Ikolo was the huge tomtom which slept in majesty inside the chief's court. Long-short, long-short; short-long, short-long; long-short ... In the more exciting days of wars with the neighbours, such beats had summoned the elders of the town to meet for some important discussion. They must all come at once, Ikolo ordered; and they should not stop on their way to talk to anybody.

Not long after, the elders began to assemble. When they were informed about the decision they applauded with vigour. They could now depart from life, they commented, nodding in contentment; in that case, they would die happily, knowing that Nade had not been allowed to burn to ashes during their time as custodians of custom.

Later that day, the decision was proclaimed in the entire town. Nobody was to join the group again and those who were there already were to repent and expiate their offence.

Midway to Idimogu's house, Chiaku shrugged once more, in horror. She reflected: 'It isn't six moons yet since the rulers and elders made a proclamation! And today, Ibe, with whom Nnanna is salt and oil, has joined the gathering! I must tell Idimogu how I feel, and that in clear language. . . .'

Suddenly, she halted. She stood motionless for a few minutes and tried to reason within herself. Perhaps Oji was right, she said. It would be unwise to speak to Idimogu today. He would not have the ears to listen. She had better go tomorrow, or the day after.

She turned.

Back at the house, she found Nnanna busy restringing his bow.

'Bow and arrow every time!' she said furiously. 'Are we going to eat them? Put those things aside at once and find something to do in the house.'

'I'll soon be through,' he said casually.

'You'll soon be through with your head!' She dashed forward and wrenched the bow from his hands. 'Cruel ones, you want to ruin your mothers! Day in, day out, you keep on stringing your bow, leaving everything to me.'

He was amazed. He stared at her, speechless.

'Have you heard about your friend?'

He continued to stare.

'Have you heard or not?'

'What is it?'

'He has joined the evil gathering.'

'Is that why you should shout at me like that?' he protested.

'You ask me that?' she exploded. She glanced here and there and found a stick, a fairly big one. She picked it up. 'And you have the courage to stare at me like that – as if I were your age?' She struck him on the head.

She sat down. 'You have been associating with such a wicked creature and yet you have the effrontery to throw questions at me.'

He made a sniffing sound. She looked at him. She saw tears coming down his cheeks.

'Of course I know you will never do such a thing,' said she, relenting. 'You cannot let your mother into mortal grief.'

Nnanna stood up. He wiped the tears with the palm of his hand.

'You mustn't move with Ibe again, you hear me?'

He did not say a single word. He left her and walked out, the bow in his hand.

'Tomorrow morning I'll go and warn his parents,' she said aloud to herself.

She did not go in the morning. She had to keep an eye on him in case he should attempt to go to the place. She went in the evening instead.

She found both of them in.

TEN

She was certain she had frightened him sufficiently when she shouted at him savagely and hit him with a stick and caused tears to drop from his eyes. He would never think of following Ibe to the place. Nnanna could be difficult at times, she knew. More so of late, since his voice began to deepen and he sprouted like a yam sapling. But she could still frighten him, whenever the need arose. The instrument for that was sudden outburst, loud and furious. She must make the attack first and put him on the retreat. Every mother was supposed to know like the palm of her hand the character of each one of her children. Nnanna was her only child; she knew him even better than that ... All the same, she must observe him carefully. Especially in the hours before noon, when the place was in session.

'We'll start to learn the new dance this afternoon,' he said to her one morning.

'Which one? she asked in sudden apprehension.

'I told you that our age-grade want to learn a new dance.'

'I now remember. Where do you do that?'

'At Odunze's – Odunze who is Okaka's father. It was he who discovered the dance for us at Umueri.'

'I would like to come and see what it looks like,' she said after an interval of time. 'Will I be allowed in?'

'You will. We agreed that parents could come and watch during practices.'

'What do you say the dance is called?'

'Ukwueluani.'

She chuckled. 'Will you fly in the air then? I've never heard of it before.'

'It's new.'

'It must be. What do they charge for coming all the way from Umueri to teach it?'

'We shall each pay sixty heads of cowrie shells.'

'As much as that?'

He explained: 'Odunze will use part of it to buy the things they demand. He will give them the rest to take home.'

'Perhaps it's reasonable, in view of the distance they travel to Nade. I hope you will raise the money yourself and not wait until Chiaku pays for you.'

'I've been picking palm kernels in the bush. You can see the heap at the backyard.'

'I've seen it. You'll get it sold?'

'Yes.'

'That will not do; you'll have to pick some more before I can take it to market.'

'I will, when I have the time.'

Nnanna left the house after lunch. About two hours later, Chiaku left too.

The dancing had not started when she reached Odunze's house. The experts from Umueri still sat huddled together at one corner of the front yard. They looked like persecuted men, with sad expressions on their scarified faces. Now and again one of them would sigh and wonder aloud how a stranger, hungry and thirsty, could be expected to leap up into the air. Before them stood Odunze. He was pleading and negotiating with the leader.

'. . . The yam you've just eaten is only to start with. We've started to boil cassava for pounding.'

'And only two cups of wine for each of us so far!' moaned a wicked-looking one among them who had been pouting all the time.

'There's plenty of wine, real palm wine of bitter-sweet essence, in our land,' Odunze submitted. 'You'll have enough to drink.'

'When we have died of thirst!' answered a fierce-looking one with protruding front teeth. 'I don't know what evil spirit led me to this place!'

Another said: 'Let's go home at once.'

'Of course you can't do such a thing,' Odunze replied, gravely and efficiently. 'You can't disappoint these boys. Is that how you people behave in a strange land?'

'Hear what he is telling us!' they shouted at the leader. Most of them were opposed to his spirit of give-and-take. But he hushed them. And from that point the negotiation went on to practical details. The leader got Odunze to promise that they would have a whole goat, hoof to horn, for supper.

Then they uncoiled, stood up, and began to prepare.

The gong sounded, asking some question. The flute answered. Just forming, the dancers yelled and hurried. In a slow and sober note the flute gave the necessary instruction. They must dance very well, it said. They must create a strong impression on the learners with the very first dance. Let their faces thaw: let them dance with all their heart.

The drums began to throb – slowly at first. The tom-tom started too. The tempo rose and rose. Then the rattles and lesser instruments came in. The dancers spread out into a horse-shoe formation.

A few minutes later, the formation changed again. In fact, it seemed as if there was none at all. Wide apart, the dancers stamped their feet with convincing masculine strength. Now and then, one of them would cry or shout, calling himself a praise-name or answering to a cryptic remark from the big metal gong.

'Ukwueluani!' the flute announced.

They now started the movement from which the dance had its name. They dodge-step-and-dodged with a nimble grace. They danced forward, then backward. After that they stooped, rose, gyrated. Finally, they spun round like dervishes, and leapt up high in the air. When they landed they broke out, yelling orgiastically, and stamped their feet abstractedly on the ground. All the while, their small ankle-bells tinkled in confusion and the flute wove its hectic incitements. Then, suddenly, as if by switch action, the music and noise died. The air rang with a shallow applause from the small crowd of learners and their parents, and the dancers stood in their places, all silent and exhausted, fanning themselves.

'Come out now and begin to take the first steps,' the leader ordered. His voice was stern and it was clear that he was not going to have any nonsense.

Chiaku watched. The boys came out. They looked a carefully selected group. All of them seemed to grow as you looked. Nnanna was there. Ibe was not. She had seen all she wanted. Nnanna not only had not joined the accursed gathering, he was still interested in dancing. Which was proof that he would not join: the villains who went there were not allowed to dance.

She left them and went away. But she did not go home straight. She went to a friend to make final inquiries about Ego.

She had already inquired extensively about the character of the girl who was going to be her daughter-in-law. She felt she had inquired sufficiently now. She would suggest to Oji that they take the first step, which was to make a formal proposal to the parents of the girl.

She went to see him one day, at midday. But just as they were beginning to compare their impressions, Nnanna came in. Oji took in his features with a sly look, from the tip of the toes upwards.

'You've been growing very fast of late, my son,' he said. 'Now, grow taller still, in my presence.'

'Of course he grows,' said Chiaku with a pleasant cynicism. 'Doesn't the tail of a cow grow too? He who doesn't work for his mother is only a cow's tail: he grows downwards towards the earth.'

'Is he no longer your hero?'

'Anyway—' She turned to Nnanna. 'My husband's father, do you want to see me?'

'Yes.'

'When the grass is burnt,' Oji mused, looking at Nnanna from the corner of his eyes, 'the ground is charred and is charcoal-black. And when rain falls, the ground is soaked. And when the ground is soaked, green grass begins to appear.'

'What does all that mean?' she asked.

'You don't understand? Your son's charcoal-black skin has just been soaked with the water of manhood. If you look close you will see the result.' His big face expanded into a smile.

'He comes!' she objected.

'It's true, isn't it?'

'Did you say you wanted me?' she diverted.

'Yes,' replied Nnanna.

'Is anything wrong?'

'Somebody is in our house.'

'Who could that be?'

'A girl.'

'You don't know her name?'

'She's called Ego.'

Oji felt a terrific urge to shout. She caught his eyes. He grimaced instead and coughed teasingly.

'What has she come for? Did you ask?'

'No,' Nnanna said curtly. 'She brought you a pot of water.'

'She is a good girl. Go and stay with her; I'll soon be back.'

'She's waiting for you.' He went away.

'Of course he will not go to the house – if I know children well,' Oji said. 'Women! Nobody can predict your next move.' He laughed. 'That one is for you, my sister.'

She tried to explain: 'Nothing has been done yet, and nothing could have been done without your knowledge. I only asked her mother to tell her to bring me water.'

'I know! You've not been drinking water all these years. Why don't you admit that it's you who schemed it all?'

She did not reply.

'What were you up to?'

From the tone of the question, she was sure that he knew the answer, that he was just teasing. She had arranged that Ego should come to the house on that day and at that hour. The idea was that Ego should meet Nnanna alone, at the hour when people were very busy at work and there was great quiet in most homes. Nnanna would see the girl stepping into the yard, a pot of water on her head, her budding breasts bare and prominent, beads bouncing on her waist. Receptive adolescence would thrill at the sight and the impression would register firmly. 'Why not ask your daughter and mine to bring me a pot of water sometime?' she had said to Ego's mother in the market. Then they proceeded to fix the day and even the hour. That was the usual way: it began with a pot of water, or a bundle of firewood, or fodder for goats, from either side.

Ego was busy scrubbing the floor when she came in. On her own initiative possibly, she said in her mind; more probably, it was inspired by her mother – if she knew her fellow-women well! Kneeling on both knees, Ego rubbed and scrubbed with all her teenage strength, and the waist-beads danced, and her whole body, with its luscious, ripening flesh, shook.

'Thank you, my good daughter,' she said. 'Where is that mad one called Nnanna?'

'I don't know,' Ego replied disinterestedly and went on scrubbing. 'He went out.'

She had already had a hint! This was only customary modesty: every girl must behave as if she did not want to hear anything about the suitor. 'He wouldn't tell you?'

Ego merely shook her head and continued to scrub.

Silent, Chiaku studied the features of the girl that was to be her daughter-in-law. Yes, she was the right type, she said in her mind. Just the age. She was tall and erect; therefore she would produce tall children, Nnanna being tall too. The hip was broad; therefore she should not find child-bearing difficult. She had a healthy look; she would not bore her husband to death with complaints about pains here and bites there.

'The jigida which you wear looks very nice. Stand up and let me see.'

Ego stood, facing her.

Chiaku ran her downwards, starting from the girl's chest. Then she pulled the beads outward, towards herself. At once Ego recoiled and froze. A few seconds later, she began to rub her eyes with her left wrist, shielding them, most imperfectly, in the process.

'Thank you, my daughter, for helping your mother to tidy the house,' said Chiaku. She left the beads. The girl was virtuous – she was probably untouched. . . . However, you couldn't be too careful, the elders told you again and again, as if that was the refrain of a wife-hunting hymn. It should take many moons, even years, of discreet inquiries and observation. You inquired from someone, who in turn inquired from someone, and so on, closer and closer to the family of the girl, until the thing got to the parents' ears. Marriage was a very important matter; therefore it must not be rushed. It was only at the end of your inquiries, when you had satisfied yourself that the road was clear, that you could discuss it face to face with the other side.

Three months later, Chiaku was ready to talk it over face to face with the girl's mother. But before that, she should consult Oji again.

'Shouldn't we begin to approach them about the girl?'

'I thought you had already begun.'

'Without your knowledge?'

'I was only asking,' Oji apologized. 'Have you satisfied yourself now?'

'Very well.'

'So have I,' said he. 'The road is clear. Go and hint to her mother first. If she consents then the matter is as good as successfully concluded.'

Days passed. It was early morning, the time when, a people said, very important matters should be discussed before the heart is poisoned by the sad happenings of the new day. Chiaku set out, cutlass in hand. Ego was busy sweeping the yard when she arrived. Ego's mother was cracking the hard shell of palm nuts for the kernel.

'Good daughter, you sweep very well.'

'Doesn't she?' the mother concurred. 'You wouldn't believe she's already been to the stream this morning.'

'I shouldn't be surprised, knowing her to be a very industrious and obedient girl.'

She sat down on a dwarf stool, near the outer fringe of the floor.

'I'll enter your bush for fodder on my way home; if you don't mind.'

'I mind, why not?' the other answered. 'Don't you know that your sister eats fodder?' She paused. 'As if this is Ossa on a hill where they watch their scanty bush like a treasure house!'

'Or perhaps my daughter will do that for me,' Chiaku requested.

'She will. Ego, please help her to cut some fodder. You can leave off sweeping for the moment.'

As soon as Ego had gone out, Chiaku began:

'We women don't know how to speak our minds in proverbs. I shall tell you in very plain words what I've come for.'

The nuts ceased to crack. Ego's mother put the stone aside, swept the shell aside. She sat upright, pulled her legs together and gathered her loin cloth into her lap. Chin in hand, she beamed inquiringly at her visitor and said:

'What is it, my sister?'

They looked steadily into each other's eyes.

'It's about this your daughter.'

'Yes?'

'I like her.'

'How?'

'I want to take her away.'

'I don't understand you yet.' There was a big frown on her face.

'Don't devour me yet, please,' Chiaku said. 'You speak as if you are all that naïve! This is it then, in a straightforward style. I want her for my son, Nnanna.'

'Is that it?' She relaxed. She smiled a non-committal smile. Then she offered her visitor snuff, thus bringing the whole thing to an amusing anti-climax.

In the middle of the snuff, Chiaku asked:

'Did you hear what I told you?'

'I thought I did.'

'What do you say then?'

'What do you want me to say?'

There was a silence.

'May I cook breakfast for you?' asked Ego's mother.

'No, my sister. Thanks. I've something to do at home and must be going. I could come back tomorrow or so.'

'You'll be welcome. Perhaps you'll stay and eat when you come.'

'Till then. But it may not be tomorrow – in fact, it cannot be. I think my brother Oji should come and speak to Odu before. Let it not look as if we women are arranging for a marriage without the men knowing.' She rose.

'As you please. Do you really mean to go now?'

'I must. I shall see Ego on my way and take the fodder she has collected. Think seriously about what I told you, please.'

'Go well.'

In Odu's living room there were assembled a party of twenty, eight of whom were members of his extended family. Among the rest were Oji, Chiaku and Nnanna. A mild rain was falling, entirely out-of-season. Darkness had set in but it was not yet supper time. The party drank and conversed while rain-drops drummed on the mat roof.

When the rain ceased, Oji clapped his hands and drew attention to himself. He said:

'I greet everybody!'

'Same to you!' they responded.

'We've come on a specific purpose. That rain which has just stopped is a rain of blessing; the journey we've made to Odu's house this night will prove a happy one.'

'Iweadinobi!'

'May it be well with you all! Odu, my friend and age-grade, what a man cannot eat he must not keep for himself. That is a proverb as well as a statement of fact. There's a fruit we have found in your farm. Fortunately for us, neither you nor any of your kinsmen can eat it. We on the other hand love that fruit very much and wish to take it away.'

Odu answered: 'When darkness has fallen on a discussion proverbs should be eliminated. Perhaps you could come out plain, Iweadinobi.'

'Your words are very clear to me,' Oji said. 'The fact is this: Nnanna there' – he indicated with his eyes – 'who is my sister's son has brought some coconut for Ego your daughter. If you call her out for us Nnanna will present it.'

It took Ego well over fifteen minutes to arrive from her mother's house which was within the compound. Even then, her face was drawn as if she had come to give battle. Odu beckoned and she went and knelt by his side.

Silence descended upon the gathering.

'Go on,' said Oji to Nnanna, in almost everybody's hearing. 'Stand up and take it to her.'

Nnanna stood up. He advanced, a coconut in hand. But when he had only two or three more paces to go, Ego turned her back on him.

Then Odu exercised his prerogative as the father. 'Turn round, Ego, and accept the coconut,' he instructed. 'Between us and them there is no barrier. Is that not so, my kinsmen?'

'Very true!' they confirmed.

Ego hissed disgustedly before she turned. So her mother had emphasized while coaching her for the great occasion. She must behave as if she hated the whole idea – hated to think about leaving her parents to live with a man. Such behaviour, far from being disappointing, would help to confirm the impression that she was a virtuous girl. Her face averted, Ego stretched out her hand and wrenched the coconut from Nnanna's hand. And with that the formal betrothal began.

Later that night, when Chiaku had the leisure to reflect upon the visit to Odu's house, she tried to list the important things still to be done before the bride could come home. They were: countless jars of palm wine for Odu and his kinsmen; the bride-price; the various rituals; and finally, the ceremonial marriage-outing. There was no hurry. Nnanna was just a little over fifteen years old. He had not yet been initiated into masquerade cult; he would be before the next harvest season. There would be no harm at all if the marriage programme took as many as three or four years to complete. That would leave sufficient time to study the girl more closely still; and to save bags of cowrie shells for the bride-price. 'Many are the days between acceptance of coconut and marriage-outings.' That was not only a common saying of the land. It was a statement of fact.

ELEVEN

The day was nkwo – the market day of Nade. The time was afternoon. Nnanna, alone in the house, was peeling off into threads the skin of yellow, tender palm fronds. The threads were to be woven into ankle-wear for the new dance.

'Hoi!'

He started and looked up. 'When did you come in?' he asked, smiling.

'Day before yesterday,' replied Ibe humorously.

'I have been expecting you for a long time now. You told me you would come in immediately after she had left for market.'

'I decided to go to the market first.'

'What for?'

'To make sure she was there. I don't want anybody to grind my feet in a mortar; or to cut off my lips with a knife.'

'I'm sorry for you then.'

'Why?'

'Because she is hiding inside the house.'

'Shut up! I saw her in the market before coming, and I came straight.'

'We had better go to the backyard. Let me bar the entrance door first.'

They moved to the backyard. There Ibe asked:

'What are you doing with those raffia threads?'

'They are for the new dance. By the way, you've missed the dance. It's very good indeed. We all enjoy it.'

Ibe clucked in disdain. 'I'm not interested.'

'Do you really mean to continue going to that place?' Nnanna asked.

'I do. I like it very much. The school in particular.' This was where they had got to the last time they met – four days before.

'So you won't dance again?'

'No. Master says that it's sin; we mustn't take part in dances.'

'Who do you say said so?'

'Master.'

'Who is he?'

'You don't know?' he bluffed. 'That's what we call the teacher.'

'Is that his name?'

'No. It's English – white man's language. It means a man who is at the head. Master teaches us many things.'

'Like what?' asked Nnanna interestedly.

'There are so many,' the tempter said with some elation. 'For example: one, two, three, four, five.' He pressed down the fingers as he counted. 'You know what they mean?'

'Tell me.'

'Ofu, abua, ato, ano, ise. That's the one we learnt today in school. It is the way they count in white man's home. We also learn to speak like the white man.'

'Have you learnt to speak already?'

'Some. You want me to speak for you?'

'Go on.'

'Listen then; let me say the one we learnt just yesterday: There is a very fat cat on the mat.'

'Fri fri fri cat cat mat mat,' Nnanna mimicked, smiling. 'What does it mean?'

Ibe translated.

Nnanna was quite impressed. 'Have you learnt other things besides?'

'A lot. Did you know that all those who go to school will one day be great men in the land?'

'Who said so?'

'Master did. They will work for the District Commissioner, for which they will be paid some amount of money whenever the new moon appears.'

Nnanna gazed.

'When I was preparing to join,' Ibe went on, 'I told you I wasn't sure I would continue. I am very sure now. I like the place very much. Go on with your dances and masquerades and things; Ibe is no longer interested.'

'You are joking!'

'Let it be. I haven't told you that I can now write my name!'

'How do you do that?'

'Look.' He wrote on the ground. The letters were bold, fairly well-formed; but the spacing was irregular and they were out of alignment. Ibe had made a good start in the school and the teacher had already spotted him as a possible talent. 'That's my name,' he said, then spelt. 'Every one of us knows how to write his name.'

'You must be learning a lot of interesting things there,' Nnanna remarked with a faint hint of regret. 'Can you write my own name too?'

'Easy.' He bent down to write. The first sound baffled him. Two letters, n and u, contest it in his mind. He awarded it to the latter and wrote *Unauna*.

Nnanna tried to reproduce the writing. The letters he formed were almost irrecognizable. Ibe laughed patronizingly and said:

'You have tried.'

'You'll teach me again next time. Let's go out and hunt.'

'That's one of the things I've come to see you about,' he objected. 'Master says we should keep away from those who are not members – they are pagans while we are Christians.'

'Do you mean that you are going to keep away from me?'

'It's difficult,' he confessed; 'but it isn't my fault. However, I shall ask Master to allow me. When I come next time I'll let you know what he decides.'

'When will you come again?'

'Next market day – when she will be away from the house. I mustn't stay longer than this. See me off.'

'I won't. It's better you go out alone.'

'Goodbye then.'

He left the house noiselessly and disappeared into the nearest bush. That evening he went and reported to Joseph how far he had gone in converting Nnanna.

He came again on the following market day.

'Master says I may play with you,' he said. 'Provided you do not drag me to your dances and other things. And he would like you to come and join us.'

'How does he know me?'

'I told him all about us. Will you come?'

Nnanna evaded: 'Have you learnt any new things since then?'

'Yes, of course. We learn something new every day.'

'Tell me some.'

'Where do I begin?' he asked himself aloud. 'Let me speak English for you.'

'Go on.'

'I am a little boy.'

'Meaning?'

Ibe translated. 'Listen to another one: My name is Ibe Idimogu.'

'You gave your name, and then your father's. What does that mean?'

He translated, after which he explained why he should mention both his name and his father's. 'That is English,' he said. 'There's another one we call Arithmetic. Like' – he said in English – 'two times three, six.'

Nnanna stared as if in a trance. A sense of inferiority had begun to come into him. Before he would utter a word, Ibe went on.

'Master also teaches us about God. We who go to church will enter a happy place when we die, provided we do what God commands.'

'Die now and go to the place, whatever it is!' said Nnanna. 'Which God do you mean?'

'The only true one. He lives in heaven above. Heaven is the happy place to which good men go when they die.'

'Igwe?'

'No!' Ibe exclaimed – so grievous was the blasphemy! 'He is up above but not your Igwe. Those who do bad in this world He will throw into fire when they die. And those who refuse to come to church do bad. They will be left in the fire to burn for countless years.'

'Shut up. That one is your own invention.'

'So you think. When the fire begins to burn you, you will know that what I say is true.'

'It will burn you, not Nnanna.'

'It won't be my fault.'

'May it burn you to ashes. I don't want to come, if that is what you want. Go and learn whatever the man teaches you; I'll stay at home ...'

They made it a habit to meet on market days, at the hour when the market was supposed to be at its peak. Sometimes they would go into the bush to hunt in secret. There Ibe would tell Nnanna more about the school and Nnanna would listen with great interest, only to reject all his suggestions abruptly in the end. Then, one day ...

Chiaku had left the house shortly after breakfast for Umudiobia where a daughter of the family was reported bereaved. Nnanna thought she would not be back until late in the evening. Ibe assumed that she had gone to the market as usual. They were conversing freely in the frontyard when a voice asked:

'Who are those talking in the house?'

They were transfixed.

She stepped in. She gasped. When she recovered her breath she said:

'I had thought so. Friendships don't break up so easily; you must have been meeting unknown to me.' Her voice was deceptively calm.

They stood up and looked on, confused and speechless.

'The devil thing they call Ibe, I've caught you today!' she burst out. She stepped towards him. She cursed, pointing: 'May thunder strike you dead if you come here again!'

They separated.

For some moments she stood silent and motionless. It seemed as if she was mustering all the energy in her for a vio-

74

lent spring. Then she raised her hands and arched them over her head. The fingers were interlocked and the palms rested on the head.

'Idimogu, come and remove your son! Come and remove your son! Come and remove your son!' she cried, to the very limit of her voice. In reply to which the children of the neighbourhood shrilled:

'Who did it?'

That was a common joke on those who raised unnecessary alarm, or disturbed without good cause the God-given quiet intended for all. They were asking her to tell the world why she was crying like that. Was somebody dead? If so, was he murdered? If so . . .

She cawed: 'Idimogu, tell your son to leave my son! Tell your son to leave my son! Tell your son to leave my son!'

'Who did it?'

She crowed: 'Idimogu, take your son and leave my own! Take your son and leave my own! Take your son and leave my own!'

They hailed again.

Then, when there were no more voices in the air, Oji called:

'What's wrong, Chiaku?'

'Come here and see,' she answered. 'It's the evil one they call Ibe. He wants my son. Idimogu, please come and remove your s-o-n-oh!' she cried again.

'Who did it?' said the children.

'That's enough now,' Oji reprimanded. 'Don't set the neighbourhood aflame this afternoon. You shout Idimogu's name as if he sent the boy. Don't you know he is no less worried than you?'

She looked fiercely left and right. Her eyes caught a dry and tiny broomstick. She picked it up and walked furiously towards Ibe. Neither of the two boys could guess what she was going to do with just one small broomstick. She broke off a piece, a few inches long, and stuck it in the groove above Ibe's left ear.

'That is my ogu and I have given it to you and your parents!' she said. Ogu is the moral force, that potent spur of righteousness, who drives the innocent against his aggressor. The piece of broomstick symbolized this righteousness, and to break it deliberately would symbolize calculated aggression. 'You have come to ruin Ejimadu's daughter who has done you no wrong. Take my ogu home to your parents and let them break it. Or break it yourself.'

Ibe did not go into all that trouble. He removed the stick from his ear, profanely, and threw it away. He then walked away.

'Come here again and see if I won't crush ripe pepper into your eyes and nostrils. As for taking my son to that place, you will never succeed.'

Turning to Nnanna, she demanded an explanation.

Later that day, in the evening, she went to see Oji.

'We'll find something for him,' Oji promised. 'Something that will keep him away from the place. Anyadi can do that for us; we don't need to see Ezedibia yet.'

'You'll see to that?'

'I will. I intend to go in the morning.'

'Please don't forget.'

'I won't. My only fear is that those who go to the place seem to be baffling our priest-doctors. So many people have tried, without much success, to bring their children or relatives back. My sister, this thing is beginning to look like the bad ulcer which thrives on the very medicine you apply to it. However, they say it's all right so long as one hasn't joined yet; that the priest-doctors could keep such a one from joining.'

'It must be so, she said, wishfully, 'otherwise many more people would have joined.'

'What they find in the place Ejimadu's son doesn't know.'

'Nor does the daughter. And why should they have come into Nade first of all the towns around?'

'The thing is spreading. I hear Ozala now has it, though the one there is known by a different name. The one here in Nade is Fada; and the one there is Siemens. But they are both the same, the only difference is that the white man who is called Fada has no wife or children.'

'And he wants others' children instead! The wolf from above will cleave his body into two one of these days!'

'He surely would deserve such rough treatment,' said Oji amused.

'Please don't forget to go to Anyadi.'
'I will remember.'

He came to her house a little after breakfast time the following day. He took her aside to one corner of the yard.

'Take this,' he said, whispering, and handed over to her a yellow piece of chalk wrapped with green leaf. 'Mark the fringe of your floor with it every night before you go to bed. Do so again in the morning before you leave the house. Don't forget.'

'Forget?'

TWELVE

She sat up till late in the night slicing a potful of boiled cassava roots. Like the expert she was, she combined speed with skill, reducing each tuber to hundreds of pieces. Near her stood a small wooden tripod on which burnt a fibre candle. She would take the cassava to the stream in the morning – that was why she must not sleep until she had finished slicing.

By the time she finished it was already midnight. She heaped the slices inside a basin-like basket. She went outside. There she beat her palms lightly on the ground. Countless grains of sand adhered. She rubbed the palms together and the gluey stain from cassava came off in small pin-like rolls.

Back at the house, Chiaku went into the sleeping room. The candle was burning in her left hand. She saw Nnanna stretched out indecorously. His limbs were thrown apart, his jaws were open, and a small stream was flowing from the corner of his mouth. She was irritated. She began to arrange him. When she shifted his legs he stirred and resisted:

'No, no, no!'
'Lie well.' She pushed him.
'That thing you told me makes me laugh,' he mumbled.
'What are you talking about?'
'He ate his own share of the meat raw.'
'Which meat?'

'The squirrel we caught when we were hunting. He ate his share raw.'

'Who did?' No answer. 'You always talk nonsense in dreams.'

He began to develop a snore.

In the morning she had left the yellow chalk on the bed, under the mat. She removed it now and returned to the parlour. There she drew a wavy line along the outer fringe of the floor. She did that with both relish and devotion. She had faith in the charm – absolute faith which left no room for doubt. 'The villain will not come again,' Chiaku said in her mind. 'This has done it.' The line was thin: she must economize on the chalk.

She retired, finally, into the sleeping room. She went to the feet-end of the bed. She bent down and removed a black basket from underneath, exposing a hole stuffed with the hard and opaque skin of palm-frond stalk. She removed the stuffing and took out something – a packet.

Chiaku sat down on the bare floor and opened the packet. She counted the contents, gently as usual. The shillings were ten and the pennies were twenty. Her face contracted. She was calculating, reducing the amount to cowries. One penny was twenty heads and ten; two pennies were twenty heads in three places ... one shilling was ten pennies and two which were twenty heads in three places, in six places ... The whole amount was equivalent to four bags, or a little more. Add the two bags she had on the rack overhead. That would do for both his initiation into masquerade cult and the bride-price on Ego.

But what about other things? she asked herself. Like the expense of starting the couple off in their new home. She still had much to do. She would go to Umudiobia market on coming oye day – in three days' time; and she would take a heavy basket. For four consecutive markets now she had not been there. One relative or another had died and she had had to attend the funeral. She hoped nobody would die this time.

She tied the money back, put it in the hole and stuffed the hole as usual. There was inside the black basket a hard piece of stone just big enough to fill the fist. In this stone dwelt the spirit that guarded the treasure. She picked it up and held it before her, prayerfully, for a few moments. Then she put it back in the basket and finally left the basket over the hole.

She lay down. But for almost an hour she was wide awake wondering what produce she could take to Oye Umudiobia in three days' time. This was famine season. Crops were yet growing and there was hardly anything to sell. Except perhaps some palm-oil and kernel. She would crush the palm fruits she had and take the oil to the market. What else ... The small cock which slept only on treetops could go as well: she had two other cocks, big ones at that, and two cocks were enough for the hens. She was particularly happy about the goats. The five of them were doing very well, and the proud-looking beautiful she with white spots on its black body would probably produce within four moons or five ...

Dawn was not yet complete when she woke in the morning. She drew another line, thin and wavy, along the edge of the floor. Then she set out for the stream, the basket of sliced cassava on her head and an empty pot on the top.

Ibe arrived at the entrance door. He found it closed. He pushed. It creaked and gave to. He entered.

'Nobody inside?'

'Who?' Nnanna answered from behind, outside the compound.

'I.'

Nnanna ran in. His hands were mud-stained.

'I thought it was a thief.'

'Is that why you should pant?' Ibe said. 'You probably came to catch him! See how dirty your hands are.' He made a disdainful face.

'I was working in the farm.'

'You work until your hands are blistered red. Go on if you won't come to school.'

'You didn't go today?'

'No. Today is Saturday and we don't go to school. I thought I should visit you.'

'Suppose she sees you again?'

'Is it about the ripe pepper?'

They laughed, but with restraint.

'And the mortar; and the tapping knife,' Nnanna said.

'I saw her passing to the stream. She had a basket on her head and a pot on the basket.'

'That's correct. She took some sliced cassava to the stream for soaking before washing.'

'I've come to take you now, Nnanna,' declared Ibe.

'Go away. Haven't I told you I will not come?'

'Master says I should come and speak to you again. He wants you to join us.'

'I'll close the entrance door first.' He went and closed it and barred it, too.

'Master says you could come and see for yourself before you decide,' Ibe continued.

'Go away, I will not come.'

'Stay at home then and don't come and learn the new things others have been learning. Do you know how many we are now?'

'Who and who have joined of late?'

'Three from Ozala, two from Ujiji and two from Umudiobia. All of them came within the last five days.'

'Who are those from Umudiobia?'

'I know one of them; I don't know the other's name. The one I know is Ajuzie Obiako.'

'Short and stout?'

'That's he. He was brought by his mother's brother – just as I was.'

'I know him very well.'

'His father came to the school to remove him and Master ordered us to drive the old pagan out. We ran after him.' Chuckle. 'Then Master called us back and said: "If he comes here again to disturb I will have him sent to the District Commissioner." ' Chuckle.

'What new things have you learnt since we last met?'

'They are too many to be narrated,' Ibe said. 'I can now write the name of anything in this world.'

'Liar! How could you when you've been there only for—'

'There's a way Master taught us to do that,' he interrupted. 'We write while we spell. In that way, we can write anything.'

'What do you mean by spell?' Nnanna asked curiously.

'You can't understand,' Ibe bluffed. 'For example' – he spelt and wrote on the ground – 'Ajuzie Obiako.' Then he pronounced.

Nnanna was moved to envy.

'We learn other things,' Ibe went on as he wiped out the writing. 'Like Arithmetic, Grammar, and Hygiene.'

'Stop! I'm sure you're adding some salt now.'

'Let it be.'

There was a fairly long interval during which they talked about nothing in particular.

'Come back again after a few days,' said Nnanna ponderously. 'I haven't made up my mind yet, but I may go with you some time to see what you people do.'

Ibe amended: 'You haven't visited me for a long time now. You better come.'

'To your house?'

'Yes.'

'All right; I shall come tomorrow or the next day. Or do we meet in the bush? As we did sometimes.'

Ibe considered. 'Let's meet in Andrew's house then.'

'Andrew who is your mother's brother?'

'Yes.'

'It suits me.'

They fixed the date and time.

'I could have come to your mother's house to speak to you myself,' said Andrew. 'But I feared for you: if they meet you talking to me they may hide you away in a bad manner.'

His wife, Agnes, came in. She went and sat beside him, fondly, their bodies touching. She was a beautiful woman — that at least her many detractors would admit; and she was cheerful and lively, with plump cheeks and well-set white teeth. Twenty-two years old, Agnes would declare only twenty, having deliberately put her age at eighteen for three consecutive years.

'I was just telling Nnanna about the church when you entered,' he said to her.

'And he has agreed?' asked she.

'Not completely but he soon will.'

She rattled off:

'God is calling you, Nnanna. Leave off those things the pagans do and join His church, and go to school too. Ibe, I thought you said you two were very good friends. Why haven't you been able to convince him . . .?' Parrot was her nickname.

Women of Nade, especially the ones with marriageable daughters, referred to her as the winged bird ('which flew all the way from Ania on a river to find a mate'). Some called her esekempeli, which meant nothing in particular but in the area had become a name for the wayward and erring. It was believed to have been derived from the slippery speech and facetious manners of such women. Agnes was definitely not of the type. Her difficulty was that she was too sophisticated for her new society.

'He will come,' Andrew said in an abrupt tone. Even he found her loquacity exasperating at times. 'Go and prepare lunch for all of us.'

'Come to church please and pray to The Father, The Son and The Holy Ghost,' she persisted. 'Pray to Holy Mary Mother of Our Saviour, who was conceived without sin. Pray to the saints in Heaven.'

'Go now!'

'I've cooked *the thing* already,' she said. 'I only need to warm the soup. Don't forget to tell him about the Holy Mass and the Sacraments.'

'I remember all that.'

'And the reward which awaits believers.' She stood up and began to walk away, backwards. 'And the fire which awaits unbelievers. For all eternity.'

'Did you hear that your sex should not preach?' His patience was almost exhausted.

'Who is preaching?' she retorted seriously, as if she had been accused of sinning. 'I've only reminded you about the important facts to present.' She disappeared into the middle room, *en route* for the kitchen.

'What do you say?' Andrew asked.

'He will come,' Ibe answered.

'Let him speak for himself.'

The discomfort of indecision made wrinkles on Nnanna's face. He said:

'I can come and see what you do there. But is it the daily or the seven-day one that you want me to join?'

'Both of them, my son,' Andrew said. 'You are young and should learn to read and write as others do. When will you come?'

Nnanna paused. 'Let it be next oye. I believe Mother will go to Umudiobia market that day.'

'I'll come for you,' Ibe volunteered. 'When I come I shall call from behind the house.'

'You can arrange that between yourselves later on,' Andrew said.

Then, from the kitchen, Agnes announced vivaciously:

'It's ready now. Shall I bring it?'

'We've been waiting,' Andrew answered.

She brought a bowl of rice. The sight of the grains, as white as her teeth, with the soup spread daintily on top, sent a thrill into the boys' hearts. 'Osikapa!' Ibe whispered knowledgeably into Nnanna's ear and Nnanna fed his eyes steadily. In Nade and towns around, rice was still a new addition to the diet. So far, only the most enlightened, like Agnes, could cook it well, and to offer it to a guest was a special honour.

They both ate it with a grace befitting the honour, especially Nnanna who was tasting it for the second time in his life. Not one grain was wasted.

The day came. Chiaku left for Umudiobia market shortly after dawn. Nnanna hurried over the morning routine. He ate his breakfast. He mopped his face, washed his legs from the feet to the thigh and his hands up to the shoulders. Then he tied on a piece of cloth, the best he had. It draped from the waist down to the knees, allowing free movement of the legs.

Some whistling sound. Ibe probably, he told himself. He must not answer: the single and isolated call was the way of evil spirits. They called you and when you went out they took away your life.

The sound came again.

Nnanna went out and closed the entrance door after him. He went behind the compound where there was a cocoyam plot. There he saw Ibe moving stealthily up and down. Ibe was concealed, almost completely, by the big leaves, all blooming and in luscious green, which were spread on their stalks like miniature umbrellas.

'Ready?' Ibe asked and began to come out.

'Let's go,' Nnanna answered resolutely.

They set out. For most of the distance they kept to obscure

paths. When they saw people coming, or heard voices, they walked apart. Finally they arrived at the school. Hands joined, with Ibe leading, they entered the building. The pupils gave a resounding applause while Joseph smiled a dignified smile.

THIRTEEN

She was not yet back from market when he returned from the school that day. It was on the second day that he met her in.

'Where have you been all day?' she asked and glowered at him. 'You have been away from the house since morning and I've been looking for you.'

'I went out,' he said.

'You ought to have carried your carcass into the cocoyam plot behind and done some weeding.'

He gave a wink of resentment.

'You are turning into a useless child, Nnanna. I ought to tell you that in case you do not know.' She proceeded to recount all the evil things he had been doing in the house of late, including the way he talked to her.

'No lunch for me?' asked he.

'May the food choke you, lazy one,' she cursed. 'That's the only reply you have for what I have been saying.'

'You would have it choke me to death, would you?' he protested.

Silence.

'Please unsay the curse.'

She mellowed a bit. 'When such things happen in this house I begin to wonder when Ego will come over. I would then have somebody to help me.' She sighed. 'Did you see the boys who were looking for you?'

'I saw nobody,' he said distantly.

'They were three – Okaka and Ejike and one other. They came to find out why you were absent from yesterday's dance practice. It seems they are going to fine you.'

84

'They will pay the fine themselves,' he murmured. 'I don't want to dance again.'

'You are not dancing for me, are you?' she asked him. 'Why have you suddenly withdrawn, when you were so enthusiastic about it?'

Nnanna was about to speak when Oji came in. Oji, a man of even temper, looked sad and angry this afternoon.

'My sister,' said Oji as soon as he was seated, 'our people say that the bulge of pregnancy cannot be concealed for long'.

'How?' she asked, almost startled.

'Only a proverb. Have you asked your hero where he fought his battle yesterday, and today again?'

'It's what I was asking him when you entered. Please help your sister to check him. He does not want to work again.'

Oji opened his snuff container and fed his nostrils generously. 'A-a-ah!' he cried lustily and cleared the nostrils one after the other. 'Big name that kills a puppy! Hero, lion, heart of the mother, and so on! Did I not warn you, Chiaku?'

She was baffled. 'What is it?' she asked.

'Ask him where he went. Nnanna, tell us with your own mouth where you were yesterday and today again.'

'I went to learn like others,' Nnanna replied sharply and stepped backwards, towards the outer edge of the floor. 'I too have joined.' He sat down facing Oji but gazing at space.

'What does he say?' she asked.

'So you haven't understood? He went to the place – to the evil gathering which heaven forbids and the earth abhors.'

'What!' she cried insanely.

'Somebody who saw him came and told me,' Oji chanted.

'What!'

She leapt up and pounced upon Nnanna. A second later she had wound her hands round his neck, crushing it and choking him with her masculine strength.

'Let me go, let me go!' Nnanna managed to utter. Struggling very hard, he succeeded in unwinding the hands. Then he stood up and turned, facing her.

'Let you go, is that what you said?' She fell on him again. Like a maniac she tore at the hair of his head and twisted his ears; she tried to bend him downwards and to reach to his spine.

He forced her to disengage and he moved a few paces away.

'So that's what you decided to do to your mother?' she asked. 'So that's what you give me in return for everything?'

He averted his eyes.

She threw her head to one side. She stared at him pathetically. Holding with her hands the two breasts that had fed the wriggling, healthy babe, she stepped forward, closer to him. Then she knelt at his feet. Her arms went round his waist. She looked up at his face, and said, beseechingly:

'Is that what you decided to do to Chiaku?'

'Leave me!' Nnanna demanded.

She stiffened. She began to lift him so as to bring him down on the floor. But he tensed in resistance and his weight overpowered her.

She let him go.

Confused, senseless, exhausted, Chiaku looked right and left. Her eyes fell on the stout wooden pestle which she had had ready for grinding maize that afternoon. She picked it up. But as she was about to rush upon Nnanna, Oji intervened. Oji knew very well what a pestle in an angry woman's hand could do. Many a wife had employed that weapon to tame the husband, only to regret her handiwork afterwards.

'That will not happen in my presence,' Oji said and interposed himself.

'No, leave me to smash his skull and die myself without shame,' she resisted.

'May those words not go lower than your lips!' He caught her hand and disarmed her. 'Sit down first and I'll teach you something.'

She sat on the floor. Nnanna sat too, but some distance away. Oji returned to his seat, the pestle in his hand. There was tense silence.

'Yes, my sister, I'll teach you something,' Oji spoke. 'A proverb says that a wrestler who rushes furiously meets a terrible fall. The wise understand, while the foolish are fooled with proverbs. Cool down first and think.' He paused. 'But what would you have told his guardian spirit if you had smashed his head with the pestle?'

She bent down her head. It seemed she was looking at her breasts. Big teardrops fell from her eyes. They were tears of contrition, for she had now come to realize that she had lifted a weapon to end her son's life.

Oji fed his nostrils once more. 'Nwada's snuff, you can work wonders in a sad heart,' he rhapsodized. 'A-a-ah! Now tell me, my in-law, what evil spirit drove you to the place.'

'Nothing drove me,' Nnanna replied in an offhand manner and fixed his eyes on the wall opposite him. 'I decided to go, and I'll continue to go.'

'May that be your last speech in this life!' Oji cursed, for the first time in so many years. 'You will continue to go! Why not?' He ground his teeth.

'A man eats his sorrow in his heart,' he went on. 'I'll leave you two now and return to my house to think. Please, Chiaku, don't touch him again. Remember that the gods of the land will pursue you if you spill your own son's blood, or do some permanent injury to his body. I shall come back later to speak to him. He has just returned from the place and the man's spell has not worn out yet. Our words can do him no good now.'

When he left Chiaku broke into tears, sobbing spasmodically. But the load in her heart was such that could not be washed out by tears alone. She opened her mouth.

'No, I should not weep again,' she sang. 'Why should I continue to weep in this life where every broad road seems to end in bush? My eyes, you are both dry with weeping. Even the spring that flows does dry at times. How much more the tears in a widow's eyes?'

She folded her cloth into her lap. She ran her palm under her eyes.

'For ten good months I bore him in my womb,' she continued. 'Twenty years less two I was then.

' "The child will be a boy," his father used to say. "And I'm sure he will be my father."

'What Okafo foretold did come true in a way. For the child that was born was a boy indeed. But not entirely true, as I've come to discover. For my husband's father lived well till the end of his life.'

Thus she sang on, stiff in posture, hands on her laps, tearless. In moments of infinite joy or extreme distress, the Ibo woman would improvise a song and sing out her heart. While singing, she would dance and sway with the sinuous grace of a ballet; or tread to rhythm; or simply stare absently at one insignificant object or another. Chiaku was staring at a tender gecko on the wall as she recounted how grief, severe and ineluctable, had been dogging her steps since she went to live in Umudiobia.

'. . . I've laboured and laboured to obtain our living. What did I not suffer from Amanze and his wives! That was at Umudioba from where we fled. And yet I had to bear everything because of my child. That's the child that has gone mad now.

'. . . The day I faced Amanze and his wives! That was the day they said my son was possessed. On that day I taught them what not to do to a widow's only child. That's the child that has gone mad now.

'. . . I fled to Nade, to my father's land. Here to start life afresh and live in peace. Suitors have come and I've turned them out. I tell them I have a son who is my husband. Just because I don't want to live away from him. That's the child that has gone mad now.

'. . . And already I've found him a wife. She is a good girl and the family is obi. What will they say when they hear about this? Why do I live and not die at once?'

Outside, her voice rang with a cadence that plucked at the heart. Neighbours and passersby came in to see what was wrong, and to commiserate. Some chided her for crying so much. None of them could say for certain what had happened, but they guessed it was some serious misunderstanding between the mother and her son.

Among them was Nwanebe, Oji's wife. Nwanebe came forward and held Chiaku's head with a soothing touch. Then she wiped her face with the palm of her right hand, putting in all the filial tenderness she could summon in her. 'It's enough now,' she said. 'Don't cry again. But where is the boy because of whom you cry like this?'

Chiaku stopped crying. She rose and walked dreamily into the middle room. Nwanebe followed after her. They went further on. Then from where they were they saw Nnanna. He was leaning on the rear compound wall.

'So you are there, Nnanna?' shouted Nwanebe in anger. 'You are there while she cries herself to death? What have you done to her for which her heart bleeds?'

Nnanna did not say a word. Rather, he turned round and hid

his face. His eyes were flooded with tears. His mother's voice and the words of the song had eaten into his heart, and touched the son in him. But neither Chiaku nor Nwanebe knew this. They turned back, further hurt, and returned to the crowd.

Oji came again late in the night. By then Nnanna was deep in sleep.

'This is very sad,' he said in a very low voice, almost whispering. 'But know you this: nothing is smooth from beginning till end. Your son is handsome, strong and talented in many things. And in addition, he has been of good behaviour all these years. Hardly any scratch. I had in fact been suspecting that he was going to have one sooner or later. They begin to do things at his age.'

The words began to revive her hopes.

'Thinking back, remember he never carried bags for elders. Look at the other boys who go there. Not one of them, as far as I can see, was his father's favourite child.'

Her eyelids widened.

'Ibe for example. Idimogu never loved him much, even though he is the first son. Mainly because of the mother – Ibe sides with his mother against his father. Or Machie?'

'What should we do then?' she asked.

'I've been to Ozala. I saw Ezedibia.'

'You did?'

From the bag that hung down his left shoulder he took out a small packet done with black leather. 'I told him everything and he prepared this for us.' He handed it over to her. 'You owe him a white-feathered cock and twenty heads of cowries in three places.'

She inspected the packet. Her face brightened a bit. 'Thank you, my brother,' she said.

'Put it near his head every night and pick it up in the morning. It should turn his mind away from the place, since he has just started.'

'Then what are we waiting for?'

'I'd better do it myself for this night.' He took the back from her.

Noiselessly, Chiaku and Oji walked into the dark room. There Oji placed the packet close to Nnanna's head and knocked his clenched fists together, ritualistically. Then they went back to the parlour.

'Please don't forget to pick it up in the morning.'

'How can I?'

'Put it there at night before you sleep.'

'It's very clear to me.'

'Do so until the evil spirit is gone.'

'What about the other thing?'

'Which?'

'The chalk.'

'We don't need it any more. The packet will do.'

'What do I do with it then?'

'Give it to me and I'll have it buried.'

She went and brought it, and gave it to him.

She removed the packet at the first hint of dawn, before he awoke. Her heart almost palpitating, she watched to see if he would leave for the place. He did not, and would not even step out of the yard – not until it was mid-morning. He did not go on the following day. The third day came and passed. Chiaku and Oji concluded that Ezedibia had succeeded. Ezedibia, there was none anywhere in the world that could equal him! He had restored the boy's mind in so short a space of time and at so little a cost. They would send Ezedibia more than he demanded; they would show him that they were very grateful.

Early on the fourth day's morning they set out for Ozala, carrying four shapely yams and a pullet. This was in addition to the fee. But when they returned they discovered that Nnanna was not in the house. And he was not anywhere in the neighbourhood. It was later on, in the afternoon, that they found out the sad truth: Nnanna had gone back to school.

FOURTEEN

The next morning she went to see Ibe's parents again. She met Idimogu in his obi. He was sitting by the fireside. There had been a heavy rain earlier on in the day and the atmosphere was dull and damp. It was the type of weather that was best beguiled with maize and pear – which was what Idimogu was doing.

After a very perfunctory greeting, she went straight to the point:

'I've come to see you about your son.'

'Have some pear and maize first,' replied he unsmiling, and with a dignified tone.

She declined outright, frowning.

'You no longer eat maize?' He bit off some grains from the cob. 'Or you will not eat the one I offer?' His voice sounded like a masquerade's.

She made no reply. She looked steadily into space, her eyes radiating bitterness.

'You behave as if we were enemies, Daughter.' He bit off more maize, then some pear.

Chiaku's face tightened.

'You decline maize and pear in this cold weather?' he said. 'Rather funny! Are you afraid I'll poison you?'

'Have you not given me the worst poison ever brewed?' she answered tartly.

He laughed hollowly. 'What have I done to you, my child? Perhaps you are thinking about your son?'

'You very well know.'

He laughed again. 'Is that it? We are both in grief then, Daughter. I too have lost my son to the place.'

'Just show me the boy and I'll be all right when I've finished with him,' she demanded in reply. 'Show me that malefactor.'

'I quite appreciate your feeling.' He bit off some more maize. 'But it's neither your fault nor mine.' He bit off some pear.

'Your face is like an overcast sky. You are not being fair to me at all. This is a bad wind which has come into our land. I fear we may not be able to check it in spite of what the rulers decided last year. The worst thing about it is that children relish it – and these same children will one day be the fathers and mothers of the land!'

'So that's all you have to tell me?' she asked him. 'Please, Idimogu, show me the boy.'

He picked up another cob from the fire. He beat off the ashes, then broke it into two. He put one piece aside and began to eat the other.

'You want Ibe, you say?' he mumbled, with a touch of humour.

'Yes.'

'I'm afraid he's not around.'

She paused. 'Then tell me where he is so that I will go there to meet him.'

'I can see you really are in a hurry! Well, he's gone to the place. He left in the rain.' He swallowed. 'I fear you'll not be able to do much when you meet him. Do you know what happened to me just yesterday?'

She stared at him with interest, her countenance still far from friendly.

'I tried to frighten my son,' he confided. 'I held him by his two hands and threatened I would tie his feet to his hands and leave him folded up on the floor overnight like a criminal.' He gulped and went on with rising emotion: 'What did my son do in reply? He dug his teeth into my flesh. See . . . My own son did that. After that he threatened he would report me to the man who organizes them, who in turn would report to the white man at Ania! Of course I was forced to leave him. He ran out of the house pouring out further threats on me, his own father!' His teeth gnashed. 'That's my story, my child. But I do understand your feeling.'

He picked up the half-cob of maize which he had put aside.

'Take this, Chiaku. Between you and me there is no cause for ill-feeling.'

She still declined.

'I'll be seriously annoyed with you if you don't eat in my house, truly,' he insisted. 'You came in here angry and I can't

92

let you go away angry still. Eat the maize; I'll roast more pear for you.'

She accepted at last. For some time neither of them spoke. Their jaws worked steadily on maize and pear. Then Idimogu sighed sorrowfully and said:

'Do you know, Chiaku, I've no wine left in the house!'

'Don't bother.'

There was another interval.

'May I tell you something, Chiaku?'

'Yes?'

'A man's heart eats many sad things!'

'Anything?'

'Yes, Daughter. If I told you how I have been feeling since yesterday you would regard yourself as happy in comparison.'

'But you don't look sad.'

'I know. I am a man after all. I am surprised you didn't ask about your fellow-woman, Ibe's mother.'

'It's you I met first. I was going to ask about her.'

'You were! Well, she is not in – let me save you the trouble. And she will never return to these walls. Not while Idimogu has male part in him!'

She was bewildered. 'Why? What happened?' she asked.

'That woman is evil. I have sent her back to her father's house. Not while I live will she step into my compound again.' He pounded his chest three times in manly resolution.

'You men always find something wrong in the women you marry!'

'No, it's not that, daughter of Ejimadu,' he said. 'All right, did you know that it was she who advised Ibe to follow her brother – the one they call Nduru – to the place?'

'What!'

'It was she. She is in conspiracy with her brother. I think I should also include the parrot Nduru calls his wife – the one who flew into Nade all the way from Ania where nobody agreed to marry her. They are out to ruin Idimogu. But I have ogu against them all!'

'I can hardly believe this.'

'Why should I lie to you? It has just come to light. You probably didn't know that woman well. She is implacable; she is cantankerous; and she is pugnacious. Don't mind her good looks – even the millipede looks beautiful! Our people say that in a woman beauty of the body without that of the heart is nothing but sweetened poison. Do you know her latest deed?'

'No.'

'She went to a witch-doctor to prepare her some charm with which to end my life.'

'Incredible!'

'Yes, it is a fact, my child. She owned up before she left.'

'Why did she have to do that?'

'I can easily guess. She is most unhappy because of my three wives I like her least, even though she is the first. She doesn't seem to realize that it's only a woman's conduct which determines her place in the husband's heart. Another possible reason is her son. I did threaten some time ago, when Ibe had just joined the evil group, that I would disinherit her son. I only wanted to scare Ibe from the place. But she took it seriously and went about the whole of Nade complaining. Her final step was to get the witch-doctor to prepare a charm for her. If she could get rid of me suddenly, she and her son would inherit most of my property. They would then be in a position to treat the rest of the family as their slaves.'

She snapped her fingers and stared wide-eyed.

'The gods are always awake and Idimogu has not offended against them! They will not allow such a thing to happen to me.'

'This is shocking!'

'That's because you are a good woman. The one that used to be my wife still thinks she was doing the right thing.'

'Do you think her brother knows about it?'

'I can't say, Chiaku,' he said in a low and sad tone. 'Probably he doesn't. Nduru does foolish things but I shouldn't think he would plot against another man's life.'

She shrugged a number of times. 'What is it that children say? – "A creature greater than the beetle has entered the beetle's abode and the beetle has moved out for it." The story you've just told me is a thing greater than the beetle.'

'There I am, daughter of Ejimadu. And when I wanted to punish my son he revolted violently and bit me like a mad dog!'

'I must be going now. It's all so disappointing!'

'Isn't it? You are a good child, for you don't support evil. Of course there's no asking whom you resemble. Your mother, Ebenma, was well respected in her lifetime. Your father, Ejimadu, was a kind, prudent and most well-meaning man, although his temper did let him down on occasions. It's him you resemble in temperament while Oji took after your mother. One can't make any such good remarks about the woman I used to call my first wife. There is not one single good point about her character.'

'You certainly exaggerate. There's nobody in this world who hasn't even a single good point.'

'Tell me hers if you know.'

She made to leave. 'Good-bye now.'

He halted her. 'Listen to me before you go away. One thing I must tell you is this: do not think too much about those children. If you do, you may go mad or even die well before your time. Let them perish if they choose to, provided they don't perish with you and me and our like.'

'Thank you,' she said tonelessly.

'Greet Oji for me and tell him what nearly happened to his friend.'

FIFTEEN

It was midday. The atmosphere wore a heavy gloom. It seemed as if night was about to return, well before its time. Sitting on a low stool, Chiaku gazed out sombrely. She was worried in mind. Last night she had dreamt a very terrible dream, and this midday darkness coming after the dream filled her with strong forebodings.

It had begun with Igwe festival. This festival, held in honour of the god that ruled the entire universe, was always the grandest of the year. The one that Chiaku dreamt about was extraordinarily grand. Masquerades poured into the town in greater numbers than ever before. There were three principal types: fast-footed athletic ones which raced after equally fast-footed men, long canes in hand; smart ebuebu and ogbamgbada which danced for entertainment; and then, tall and imposing ones, few in number, which were the aristocrats of the spirit world. The aristocrats neither raced nor danced, but gave prestige to the town by their variegated colours, the delicately-poised components, and the dangerous charms they were believed to carry.

Chiaku saw Nnanna running past a small group of masquerades made up of these three types. A huge and misshapen one among them shouted his name. From the masquerade's protruding stomach which was entirely out of alignment with the rest of the body, she identified it as The Obese Rich One. Nnanna halted. The Obese Rich One crowed like a cock; it growled like a dog; and it hissed like a snake. At that signal the others encircled Nnanna and, without so much as touching his body, brought him down on the ground, face downwards. She ran at full speed, towards the spot, screaming. But before she got there, he was already vomiting blood from his mouth.

'Let him die who refuses to mend his bad life!' The Obese Rich One pronounced.

Nnanna gave out a shrill cry in a last desperate struggle for life. She touched his body. It was stiff, cold, lifeless.

It all moved with the absurd swiftness of a dream, and when she succeeded in recovering her mind from the nightmare and from sleep, she felt terribly fatigued in body. 'Nnanna!' she called out in the deep darkness and rose from the bed with a jerk. She called again. She bent down and ran both her hands over the floor. She touched the body. She shook it.

'Leave me, leave me!'

That was his voice, she said in her mind, then spat 'Tfia!' and snapped her fingers above her head. 'What a terrible dream!' she exclaimed.

'That goat loves palm frond best,' he mumbled.

She managed to laugh. 'Sleep and don't start your nonsense,' she said. 'Which goat do you mean?'

'Y-e-s.' He went off again . . .'

She had dreamt bad dreams before, Chiaku told herself, still staring into gloom. Surely. When a small girl, she dreamt that her mother was dead. Later, she dreamt that her father was killed, torn to pieces by an indescribable monster. Then one night she dreamt that she herself was dead. She was only fifteen years old then. It was the year Okafo gave her a coconut. Her corpse lay draped with leaves on a bamboo stretcher. Women thronged round weeping while her mother cried ceaselessly, bathing the corpse with a steady cascade of tears, and almost falling on it. The first thing she did when she woke in the morning was to tell her mother.

'Does it mean that I am about to die?' she asked.

'It doesn't, Daughter,' her mother replied. 'In fact, it's the other way round: anybody who dreams that she is dead should expect to live long.'

She was considerably relieved. But, only a few days later, she fell ill. She had a splitting head and felt a disgust for everything. Then, the next morning, she noticed that blood was coming out of her body. She was frightened, more so as there was no wound or scratch on any part of her entire body. What was happening to her? she asked herself. Was it the dream coming true? It was said that one died if one had no more blood in the body. Her own blood was wasting; she would dry up and drop dead. Flustered, she went to her mother and reported:

'Mother, I don't know what is happening to me.'

'How?'

'See . . .'

Her mother inspected. 'You are well, my child,' said she with a surprising smile. 'Nothing is wrong with you. It's your sign of womanhood and it should happen to every girl of your age who is well and can be a mother. I had in fact been expecting it in you for a few moons now . . .'

She still remembered the incident very well. For days after, she moved clumsily and cautiously, afraid every morning that she would die before the next morning. After that experience she ceased to fear her dreams; she would not even bother to remember them.

Today however she was extremely disturbed in mind. Why should it be so? Chiaku wondered. Had she not dreamt such dreams before? Or even worse? Something must be wrong: something was about to happen.

'Yes!' said she and nodded to herself pathetically. She sprang up from her seat and began to walk from one end of the floor to the other. Ten days before, she had lost a he-goat. Five days later, the beautifully-spotted she died too. Her brother Oji said the animals died of neglect. Oji could not explain why ten or more chickens should have died within the last two moons. Some evil spirits were out against her, steadily destroying her household. The events were all connected. The dream was only a final warning about the collapse. The day-time darkness was a prelude to it.

Rain clouds had now obscured the sky completely. There was a gentle murmur in the heavens. It was followed by a fierce flash – a long, red gash which came and disappeared with a click and a spark. Thunder boomed. The sound was deep and prolonged; it rolled and reverberated, causing some vibration on the ground.

More and more the gloom deepened. Then flashes and cracks came in quick unrelenting succession. It seemed as if a roaring inferno had broken out in the heavens between two camps, equally matched, one camp cleaving its enemy's ranks with burning sword, the other replying with a cannonade. The atmosphere remained heavy and still, with no wind to disperse the gloom, or a sudden rainbow to announce a change for good in the drama.

At last the rain came. In no time it developed into a torrent. A ceaseless spray of cold balls drummed on the ground with metallic force and the atmosphere roared and roared. Then a strong wind came. It twisted the taller trees, as if wringing their unyielding necks, while the shorter ones put up a sturdy resistance.

Chiaku sat tense with fear. Nnanna sat facing her, at the opposite corner of the parlour. They wished it would soon be over, this end-of-season storm the like of which they had not experienced for some time.

Then the break came. They thought that that was the end. Less then ten minutes later, the storm broke out again. This time it came with a furious wind. Such was the force of the wind that it tore away part of the thatch roof and deposited it some distance away.

Ten Hail Marys in time of danger. Nnanna crossed himself and began, silently. As he prayed he watched his mother.

She was behaving in a very queer manner. She looked right and left, up and down. She stared steadily at the sky with wide-

98

open eyes. There was something sinister about the lustre of her eyes. She swayed fearfully from side to side, as if she was dodging. It seemed she was seeing things – some weird shapes – up in the sky. Then she spread out her hands and broke into a song:

'Now it comes! That's the time – the last days of the rainy season. That's the time they say I was born. And that's the time I moved to Umudiobia, there to lose him and return to Nade!'

She stopped abruptly but continued to stare. She arched her hands over her head, with the fingers interlocked.

'That's the time he dropped from a palm-tree. Alas, he could have been saved, for the ground was wet and soft. But fate got the sharp tapping knife down before him. There it lay, the instrument of his horrible death. It was resting on a shrub, with its sharp point up. It pierced his side and he died on the spot. Yes, that's the time!'

'What are you saying, Mother?' Nnanna asked.

'What does it want now?' She ignored him completely. 'Tell me, what do you want? To destroy whatever is left? Tell Chiaku – please tell Ejimadu's daughter.'

'What's wrong with you?' *Hail Mary full of grace the Lord* . . .

The rain still poured.

'Yes, that dream is true.' She sprang up from her seat. She ran out, into the rain. She left the compound. She ran on and on, splashing through the flood which was ankle-deep in places. The rain stung her and flooded her eyes. But she went on, silent and unfeeling, as yet with no destination at all.

When Nnanna came out to look for her she was out of sight.

At last it had ceased to rain, although the paths were still full of debris and scourings and drips from the sodden foliage drummed mournfully on the ground. That day was Saturday. Nnanna went to see Joseph the teacher.

'Master,' he began, 'you told us that any member who is in need may seek assistance.'

'Yes, indeed,' said Joseph and supplemented with a nod. 'What is it you want?'

'Master, the rain damaged the roof of my mother's house and the walls are wet.'

'Can't your father see to that?'

He hesitated. 'He is not alive, Master,' he said uncomfortably.

'I remember now,' Joseph said. 'You've done very well to come here and report. It was such a terrible storm and must have destroyed several other houses. Let's summon the members.' He called: 'Smart!'

Smart, the servant, came at once.

'Ring the bell and summon the members. Ring as for an emergency.'

'Yes, Master,' answered Smart delightedly and went off briskly, in the manner that had won him his master's admiration and the name he bore.

The bell had been installed only two months before. The first day its peals were heard in Nade the townsmen had hurried to the direction of the sound to find out what it was that hummed and vibrated. On their way however they learnt that it was Joseph's latest prank; they turned back therefore and went home. Since then, the bell had been recognized as a fact of life. Except by the younger ones. They composed a number of mocking songs to it. The peals, said they, carried a wicked invitation to

> Abandon the farm
> Abandon the house
> And come here to learn.

Neither Joseph nor any of his pupils was moved by the songs. Day in, day out, the bell continued to peal, although only Smart, apart from the teacher himself, was permitted to ring it. And Smart was very efficient at it.

On this occasion Smart excelled himself. The peals came in slow and solemn spondees which conveyed a sense of grief as well as of emergency. Soon the members began to arrive, all in a hurry. They assembled outside the church building.

'I'm glad you've come in such large numbers,' Joseph addressed them. 'One of our members here is distressed and requires our help. The roof of Nnanna Okafo's mother's house was blown down during the tornado.'

'Then let's proceed at once,' replied someone in the spirit of those days. 'The women and girls may go home; the men will do it with the boys.'

'That's good word,' another said. 'It requires only one reply, which is action.'

From behind a certain woman announced:

'Our house was damaged too. Unfortunately, my husband is not here to speak. He is out of town.'

'And mine too!' said another, a man.

It then came to light that there were as many as five houses for them to repair. They divided themselves into five groups, mixing the boys with the men.

Darkness had already set in when Chiaku returned. She found Nnanna sweeping out the litter with one hand while with the other he held a burning fibre candle.

'From where?' he asked.

'Is this my house I am in?' she asked herself aloud.

'Welcome.'

She took another candle from the bundle that hung suspended over the fireplace. This part of the house had not been touched by the rain and the candle was still dry. She lit from the one in his hand. With that she began to inspect parts of the house.

'Yes, it's my house,' said she. 'And the roof?'

'I got it repaired.'

She turned and faced him. 'You did?'

'Some people came and helped.'

She stood at one spot and contemplated him. Her heart was possessed by contrasting emotions – love, gratitude and pride on the one side; disappointment and grief on the other. She sighed. Her sense of loss was accentuated by this latest demonstration of Nnanna's virtues and capabilities. She was once again reminded about the night when he rescued her from Amanze and his wives.

'Thank you, my son,' she acknowledged. 'I know you will never allow your mother to perish, whatever happens. You didn't cook for them?'

'No; I didn't.'

'You couldn't have. I shall cook for them one day. Who are they?'

'They are our members.'

'Who?' she asked nervously.

'Churchmen.'

Her face fell. The sinister lustre began to come back to her eyes.

'But where were you all the time?'

'Where was I?' she repeated, wearily, abstractedly.

'Yes.'

'Where do you think I was?'

They were both silent.

'I ran away.'

'Why?'

'To avoid you,' said she.

SIXTEEN

She had run on and on until she was tired and began to walk. When the storm ceased and her senses began to come back she realized that she was in Ozala. She decided she might as well go and see Ezedibia than whom none was greater.

She managed to find her way to the famous priest-doctor's house. There she sighed with relief, like one lost in a jungle who had just come upon the obscure track that led to light. Shortly after, still dripping, she stood before the priest-doctor in the small one-room outhouse that was his office, and narrated her case.

'Please, father, come to my rescue at once,' she implored in the end. 'His offence has drawn the anger of the gods upon my house.'

'I know your trouble,' Ezedibia replied in his usual slow and small voice. 'Your father, Ejimadu, was a good man – I knew him well. Oji your brother is a good man too. Your late husband did not offend against the gods. Just as you have said, it's your son that did it and nobody else. He has brought all this upon you. But surely such request as you make should have come from a man.' His sunken eyes glinted through the eye-lashes and focused on her forehead.

'Forgive, father, if I've erred,' she pleaded.

'If you would ask your brother to see me about the matter,' said he thoughtfully, 'I could arrange to be there before it's too late.'

'I certainly will.'

'Go back now and do as I say.'

All this Chiaku narrated to Oji the following day. She asked him to go to the priest-doctor at once. Oji tried to argue. She shouted and cried and threatened to end her life for him if he didn't. Oji gave in and promised to go early in the morning.

By noon the following day she came to hear his story.

'You saw him yourself and he promised with his own mouth?' she asked as if doubting his story.

'I did,' he assured her. 'He will be here on next afo day. I shall tell you the details later.'

'And you believe he will come?'

'Certainly. He is a truthful man – and he has to be, otherwise he would not be having so much good luck with the gods. That man is a spirit itself, believe me, my sister. Have you heard what he did recently?'

'Tell your sister.'

'So you haven't? Ozala has been infested by robbers and thieves for some time now. Last moon a gang climbed over the compound walls of the chief's residence and carried away a good quantity of yams and cattle. So he retained Ezedibia to find out for him who the villains were. "They will come again, those very people," Ezedibia said after studying his medicine pot. And do you know what happened?'

'Please go on.'

'They came.'

'They did?'

'Not only that. While they were gathering the yams in the dark night, something which Ezedibia planted there in the barn commanded them to stand still. The next morning they were all apprehended.'

'What!' she exclaimed, pleasantly amazed.

'Ezedibia! There's none to compare with you!' he rhap-sodized.

Her face lit with rising hope. 'That man does things,' she commented.

'He is great and he is dependable.' Oji expanded. 'He has done some incredible things. I remember the day he filled a small basket with palm-wine and carried it about, from one end of the market to another, without a single drop escaping. That was at Ozala, the day he said he was teaching some itinerants from Ndikeli that he, Ezedibia, was enough for all the towns around, and that there was no need for the services of empty-headed and open-mouthed ones like them.'

'I think I heard about it.'

'You must have. There was another incident in which he stood a long stick in a pot of clean sparkling water and went away. When he returned he dipped his hand into the pot and picked up a number of things – pebbles, charcoal pieces, a dead rat and some insects. The enemy had shot those poison-bearing objects at a client and Ezedibia's stick trapped them all and buried them in water.'

She listened spellbound.

'And quite recently,' Oji continued, 'he followed the scent of a poisonous snake until he found the tiny green string peering from a treetop.'

'Is he not also the one who they say once set water on fire?' she said.

'He is. That was the day he was angry and wanted everybody present to understand that he is not an ordinary man. Believe me, there's none in this world who is like him. By the way, do you know what happened to the first one we had from him?'

'Yes?'

'You destroyed it.'

'How?'

'A woman's hand should not have touched it – so Ezedibia told me today.'

'But you didn't tell me.'

'I didn't. That was his fault: he didn't tell me – not until today.' He paused. 'We may have to mortgage our father's land to pay the fee this time!'

'What does it matter if we sell ourselves too?'

He laughed. 'I don't know about you, but I'm sure nobody

will offer thirty heads of cowrie shells for me. Anyway, how much have you in your house?'

'Not much.'

'I know. It's never much. You women will never let anybody know how much you have – not until something forces you to bring it all out.'

'How much did he charge?'

'Not much. Two bags of cowrie shells – he does not want any metal – plus three goats and as many fowls as he cares to demand.'

'Isn't that too much?'

'You are panic-stricken? And yet you were prepared to sell yourself!'

'I'll try my best,' Chiaku resolved aloud.

Ezedibia arrived in Oji's house at the hour when the punctual tapper usually began the evening round of the palms. He was unaccompanied and brought with him only his bag, the inside of which no woman could see without danger to her eyes, and his black metal staff. It had taken Ezedibia well over two hours to travel from his house in Ozala to Oji's compound, a distance of scarcely two miles. That was mainly because he had to move circumspectly all the way, keeping to the left fringe of the footpath, since part of his strength was supposed to lie in the fact that nobody passed him on the left. At times he would stab and probe the bush on his left with his staff, in case some miscreant lay there concealed. Now and again he would spit on the ground or mumble to himself, or shout at the air. He was a tall and spare man, over sixty years old. His face was severely wrinkled, suggestive more of a deep mind than of age. There were people who believed that Ezedibia would live scores of years more; that his soul was securely riveted to his body by the great spirits whom he served. Some said he died and resurrected once a year, each time rejuvenated. This evening he wore an old straw hat which was bleached by fire smoke and stuck with feathers. His eyelids were painted white. He had a small bell on each ankle.

There was a third bell, the one that was tied to his staff. When he had stepped into Oji's compound he shook the staff with great force and the bell jangled.

Oji came out from the forehouse. He greeted:

'Chief among his type!'

'My child!' Ezedibia answered with an air of condescension.

'It's you we call Ezedibia!'

'May it be well with you!'

'You have proved yourself worthy of that name!' Ezedibia was only his title-name. It meant that he was chief among all dibias, men who by the nature of their profession were priests as well as doctors. (Diseases, whether of the mind or of the body, were caused by spirits; therefore anybody who professed the medical art must also be a priest, an intermediary between spirits and men.)

'Your voice is good, my child,' he acknowledged.

Oji took him into the living house.

Two men, both apprentices, arrived later. They brought the tools and ingredients for the work. On Ezedibia's direction they put down their loads at the backyard of Oji's living room. Then they began to lay out the materials – animals, vegetables and minerals – on the ground. That over, they went away.

Then from his bag Ezedibia took out a roll of animal skin spotted black and white. He spread it on the ground close to the materials and sat down on it. Close by, a fibre-candle was burning. With his practised fingers he began to pick the formulas. By the time he had finished the night was already far advanced. He put the formulas inside two clay pots. Then he spilled the blood of a cock and a hen into each pot.

It was a little after midnight and it was very dark. The sky was almost completely bare of stars. The atmosphere was still. It was that notorious hour which in the rural calm struck terror into the heart of even the most daring, when robbers feared to operate and the gipsy found shelter in the nearest hut. This was the time that witches and spirits of the dead took possession of the world.

In the backyard Ezedibia and Oji sat and conversed in low voices.

'Have you given me all that I want?' asked the priest-doctor, business-like.

'Nearly. There remains only a goat.'

He made a stern face. 'What do you say? Have you not

106

brought only two cocks and two hens – which I used for these pots here?'

'May I seek to know how many more fowls are required?' Oji pleaded meekly.

'There is something else besides fowls. I charged two bags of cowrie shells, didn't I?'

'Yes, there it is.'

Dramatically the tone of his voice changed. It was now compassionate. 'I know it's not easy to bring out even half a bag – much less two bags,' he said. 'All the same, we want this thing to be done successfully. The two bags will not do; you will have to find a third. There's something I didn't foresee at the beginning, and that is: I will have to sacrifice to the gods on her behalf every oye day. Each sacrifice will require some amount, to be offered to the gods.'

'Of course so long as you succeed, we will do our best to pay. But, Ezedibia, could you waive this extra bag? My sister has suffered so much for this boy; she has already emptied her house.'

He shook his head. 'You seem to have missed the point. We require the extra bag for offerings, without which there can be no success.'

There was an interval. 'So long as you succeed—' Oji said.

'When it comes to that I'll only repeat what I told you the day you came to see me at Ozala. The case of people who have already joined the gathering is beyond me – and beyond any dibia in this world. One could perhaps try at the initial stage, but once that stage is passed, it becomes hopeless. I am an honest dibia; I must tell you the truth. Do you understand me?'

'I hear you well. And I very well remember you told me the same thing when I came to your house.'

'I told you much more than that,' said he in the confident tone of an authority. 'I said I would work on the mother instead, didn't I?'

'You did.'

He muttered something incomprehensible. 'This thing started long ago, my child. To be definite, it started when Okafo, her husband, died. Was he not the one who dropped from a tree and was pierced by a knife?'

'He was.'

'Since then, your sister has put her whole heart on that child. Which is a dangerous thing: one must not hang one's heart on a thing that breathes, much less on merciless, changing youth. What if he had died?'

'You will live for ever, Ezedibia, for you are a wise and truthful man. All that I have already told her. Not once or twice, but many times.'

Ezedibia grinned from cheek to cheek, exposing his almost toothless jaws. 'You it is who will live for ever, not Ezedibia,' said he humorously. 'You don't want me to go up like others so as to return reincarnated? However, that's not our business for the moment. We are on the condition of your sister.'

He paused, with great effect.

'Her mind is wounded, but not incurably as yet. Are you listening?'

'Very well indeed. All that is well-known to me. The thing comes into her once or twice each day. While it is on, her eyes shine as if she is after somebody's blood. Fortunately, she is not violent; and more fortunately still, she is not yet beyond your art.'

'I will do my best,' said the priest-doctor with some modesty. 'One thing is certain: if something is not done now she will get worse and worse until she becomes permanently insane. This is Ezedibia's word and Ezedibia is a messenger of the gods.'

Then from his bag he took out a small packet done in black leather. He untied it and revealed two white tablets, as big as palm kernels. 'Dissolve these in cold water and give her to drink,' he said and touched the tablets to his tongue. 'Do that any time tomorrow and see that she drinks them down.'

Next, he took out a red-earth ball, well hardened and painted white, just big enough to fill a pair of cupped hands. 'Bury this close to the plant in which her guardian spirit dwells. Do that secretly and don't leave suspicious marks.'

'How deep?'

'As far down as you dig to bring out a big yam tuber. As from tomorrow I shall begin to make offerings to the gods. For how long that will continue will depend on your coming to pay the remaining bag of money. There are also one or two more things I'll give you, but that will be after you have sent the goat and some more fowls.'

108

'I shall come within a few days,' Oji promised.

'It's up to you. Well now, let's go and bury these pots inside her compound. Did you dig the holes as prescribed?'

'I did. There are two of them, one on the right side of the door and one on the left.'

'Correct. Bring the pots.'

But for the occasional glow of worms and flare of flies, the night was absolutely dark. Even insects seemed hushed by its density. Only the owl could be heard screeching as Ezedibia and Oji, two moving lumps of darkness, walked on to Chiaku's house. Owls went with spirits, reflected the priest-doctor; the screeching was auspicious.

When they arrived they went to one corner of the frontyard, close to the compound wall. There Ezedibia stood his staff erect on the ground and prayed in silence. After that, he asked Oji to put the pots down which Oji did.

Ezedibia stood over the pots and prayed again.

Whop! The contents of one of the pots caught fire. The flame developed steadily, until it had become a big, red ball. Then it began to diminish, in both size and intensity. Finally it vanished completely. All that took a few seconds.

'We'll now bury the pots,' he said. 'Bring them.'

They went to the holes. There he took over the pots and interred them, one after the other. With his small and wizened feet he swept back the earth into the holes until he had covered the pots completely.

'Help now to fill up the holes,' he whispered.

Oji joined him. They filled the holes to the brim. Then they trod on the top as hard as they could, after which they filled up and trod again. When they were satisfied that the earth could sink no more, Ezedibia went and lifted his staff. They left the compound and returned to Oji's house.

SEVENTEEN

In the small goat-shed at the right side of the frontyard, the one remaining goat was bleating helplessly.

'Bleat to death, beast!' Chiaku answered. 'You've rejected the palm-leaf I tied there for you. Do you want yam instead?'

The animal bleated more fiercely still, as if incensed by her voice.

'Go on,' she added; 'bleat until you die like others before you.'

Outside the compound a sympathizing voice, of a woman, said:

'Perhaps the rope has entwined round its neck and it's now being strangled. Is there nobody in that house?'

'Who speaks?' Chiaku demanded.

The entrance door was open. The woman, Ego's mother, came in. 'So there's somebody in?' said she in an outraged tone and veered to the shed. 'What's wrong with it?'

'Don't ask your sister,' Chiaku replied. 'It doesn't want to eat palm-leaves: it would rather have Chiaku's flesh. Let it bleat until it has exhausted all its breath.'

'I guess it's made with hunger.' She entered the shed. The goat stampeded, straining at the tether. Then it sniffed as if sampling her from a distance. 'Yes, it's hungry and skinny, Chiaku,' she pronounced, still in an offended tone. 'You have not been feeding it well. And besides, the shed has not been cleared for a long time now. Just look! It's like a refuse dump. This goat will surely die if you continue to neglect it the way you have been.'

'That's entirely its business,' replied Chiaku from the house. 'Let it chew its cord if it doesn't want palm fronds. And if it chooses to die, let it go ahead.'

'I'll go out and get a few leaves for it.' She left the shed. 'I guess you've been feeding it on palm fronds alone for days. Goats are like human beings, in that they don't like to eat the same thing day in, day out, from morning till night. Give me a knife and I'll go into the bush.'

'There's one there' – she pointed – 'if you want to take the trouble.'

Ego's mother picked up the knife and went out.

She brought on her return a rich variety of twigs tied together with hard creepers, at the sight of which the animal went mad, sniffing ferociously and straining with all its strength. . . . At last the fodder came within its reach. It fell to at once, and only with the greatest difficulty did she manage to tie the bundle to the rope which hung down from the bamboo rafter.

'Its cry nearly rent my heart,' she said when she had returned to the house.

'Thank you, my sister,' Chiaku said in reply. 'You have quenched the fire and it will no longer cry.'

She sat down. 'Ego sends greetings.'

'How is she?'

'Very well indeed.'

'I know you do look after her. You should have brought her with you to see her mother.'

There was an interval of silence.

'I've actually come to talk to you about her. It's painful to me what I have to say, but it must be said.'

'Go on then. Don't hesitate.'

'I want to suggest, my sister, that we have waited long enough. You know what I mean.'

'I asked you not to hesitate.'

'Many people are asking us about her, and that nearly every day.'

'Why speak to your sister in such vague language?'

'Well, they want her for their sons. And if we don't take advantage we may miss these most eligible years – which, as you know, is a bad thing for any girl.'

Nearly five minutes passed before Chiaku replied:

'I understand you well. And I can't blame you for the decision. We ought not to delay the good girl any longer.'

'I'm glad you do see with me.'

She spread out her hands in a gesture of capitulation. 'I've done my best to make my husband's father change,' she moaned. 'Nnanna, what have I not done?'

'I grieve with you, my fellow-woman.'

'Nobody would be so foolish as to marry her daughter to such a one, especially after what the rulers decided. How had I longed for the day Ego would come over and live here!' She broke into tears. 'Please, my sister, don't make me cry again. There are no more tears in my eyes.'

'You don't know how much it pains me too,' the other consoled. 'For who could have been a better son-in-law than he? Nnanna has in him the best that is required in a husband. He is tall; he is handsome. He is strong; he is a wrestler. And other things. I've missed having an in-law who could have worked for me and made me rich in crops.'

Chiaku sobbed and tears came from her eyes in thick, quick drops. She had been reminded, once again, about her best-laid schemes, and about her vision of Nnanna as an adult which she had so gladly cherished.

'What's this you are doing?' the other scolded. 'I thought you said you had no more tears left in those eyes.'

She wiped the tears. She snapped her fingers deliriously. 'Nnanna doesn't work again! And he neither dances, nor shoots, nor wrestles!'

'That's enough!'

'A tall man, well-proportioned, handsome!' she recounted, listlessly and in self-mockery. 'Of course he still is. But then, what about other things?'

'Will you shut up, Chiaku!' said Ego's mother, sternly. 'Look, I don't like the tone of your speech. Nor that lustre in your eyes.'

'What else do you want your sister to do? I can at least say it out before it chokes me to death.'

'No, don't speak like that again, or I'll be seriously annoyed with you. Our people say that nobody is another's chi – Nnanna is not your chi.'

She groaned.

'You can never tell what your chi has in store for you.'

'My chi!' Her cheeks contracted into a self-mocking smile. 'Tell me, what have you in store for me?'

'Are you mocking at yourself or what?' objected the other with a frown.

Chiaku went silent, like a child who had calmed down under a rebuke. She joined her hands at the back of her neck, with the

112

fingers interlocked, and looked on. Her countenance and posture suggested that she was now prepared to listen to reason.

'Listen, why don't you start life afresh?'

'How?'

'By marrying again.'

'What?'

'I said you should marry and start life all afresh.' The tone was firm, compelling.

She wiped her face with the left palm. She sat upright, her hands down on her lap. 'Did you say I should marry again?' asked she with a childlike candour.

'I do.'

Silence.

'Go and marry and start afresh, Chiaku. You can't continue to stay in this house with melancholy as your only companion. Perhaps you don't know that you now look worse than a vulture thoroughly beaten by rain.'

She smiled feebly. 'Who would propose to your sister at this age?' asked she rhetorically.

'What do you mean? Can't your womb still carry and your breast still feed a child? Nnanna is your first-born after all.'

She nodded.

'And in addition, you are a very good woman, as everybody in the land knows. You are wise and you are righteous. In spite of your many years as a widow, nobody can say you did this or that. I'm sure good men will rush for you if it is known that you are now prepared to remarry.'

Another interval of silence followed.

'What do you say?'

'I've heard you,' Chiaku said.

'That's not enough: you must be persuaded too.' She rose. 'I want to go.'

The goat bleated.

'Tell me, what does it want again!' Chiaku wondered.

'Nothing. She's only thanking me on your behalf. Even a goat knows that I've given you very sound advice.'

They both laughed.

'Promise you will consider it seriously.'

'Say something else now. Maybe you are going to be my husband!'

'You will please see me off.'

When they had come out to the open yard, Ego's mother said:

'I am a woman and therefore cannot be your husband. Somebody else will.'

'So you are still thinking about that?'

'Of course. Do you know my brother Okere?'

'Very well.'

'You should – I've no other direct brother.' She paused. 'If your ears are open, Okere wants to marry you.'

'What is she saying?'

'That's actually my main purpose in coming. Ego is secondary.'

EIGHTEEN

Igwe festival had started. Nade was now gay and noisy. But as yet the celebration featured only feasting. Children went about in small groups, from one house to another, and were entertained free and without obligation. Sometimes they would sit under shades of trees and compare their impressions of the hosts. Those were classified as wise and open-minded who put something soft and sizeable in the soup, while those who put in nothing at all were denounced as very wicked and narrow-minded. The boys wore their new small pants and the girls, their bodies painted, wore their special beads and bangles.

It was the third day of the celebration. Chiaku sat down for an early breakfast. She dipped a piece of yam, of the rare bitter type, in sauce. She raised the hand over her head and swung it round, once only, and with some deliberation. Then she threw the yam out. This was the first time Chiaku was offering to her chi since that bleak morning she ran out into the storm. It short-landed by over a yard. She sighed, penitently.

She took another piece and threw, with zeal this time. It landed within a foot. She prayed.

She began to eat. Not long after, she heard a knock at the entrance door. She looked up.

Ego was the visitor. She had a basket on her head. Her body was coloured festive brown, with a line of black dye running from her chest down to her navel. Pink beads piled on her waist and black ones on her wrist. There were metal bangles on her ankles.

Inside the house, Ego put down the basket. She took out the two pots in it. One pot was calabash; this contained the cassava fou fou. The other, of clay, contained the soup.

'Mother says I should give you this,' she said. Then she removed a small bit of the fou fou, touched it lightly on the filmy surface of the thick soup, and put it in her mouth.

'Lest I be poisoned by her?' asked Chiaku pleasantly. 'What would she want my life for?'

'She says she could not get bones to put in the soup and that you should look after your teeth yourself.'

Chiaku chuckled. 'Tell her I'll keep the scorpion I had intended for her; she should teach herself how to endure pain. Thank you, good daughter. I hope she is well.'

'She is.'

'Greet her for me when you get home.'

From the middle room Nnanna emerged. He had been preparing for school and was now ready to leave. He asked:

'Any food for me?'

There's plenty in the house,' replied Chiaku. 'Or do you still insist that you won't eat what kind people have brought to us for the festival?'

He frowned.

'Will you eat this one?' She pointed.

The pots were still where Ego had kept them – close to her feet. Nnanna turned his back abruptly on the two sins: a pagan feast and a naked female. He stood there silent for some time; then he walked out of the house, a sullen look on his face.

Less than half the usual number were in the school when Nnanna arrived. By the time the opening prayers were over, only a few more had come.

'What has happened to the rest of you?' asked Joseph gloomily.

Ibe suggested: 'Master, it must have something to do with the festival.'

'Which one?'

'Igwe, Master.'

'You mean they are taking part?'

'Not that, Master,' said Ibe. 'Masquerade races start today and they are afraid. It is said that masquerades will flog school children this year until the skin peels off.'

'Nonsense. Who said?'

'That's what people say in town, Master.'

'Nonsense,' Joseph pronounced again. 'No masquerade will try anything on a schoolboy. They are all unworthy ones who have absented themselves from school today.'

'What Ibe said is true, Master,' said another, a fat boy from Ozala whose name was Azuka. 'Except that masquerades will flog only those who have not been initiated. We here were all initiated before we joined the church; therefore masquerades will not touch us, unless we show them disrespect.'

Some shouted: 'That is not true, flesh without bones.' Some said: 'Who told you? Sit down!' The rest supported him and called upon the uninitiated to shut their mouths.

'That's enough!' ordered the teacher. Then he asked: 'How many of you say they were initiated before they started to come to church?'

About half the hands went up.

'How will they know you have been initiated? Just by looking at your faces? Azuka, it's you I ask!'

'Not that, Master,' Azuka said.

'How then?'

He hesitated. Another, taking over from him, said:

'Master, we know the masquerade leaf and can pick it if challenged.'

A buzz of protest.

'Did you say leaf?' asked Joseph.

'Yes, Master,' continued the flippant boy. 'The masquerade leaf which everyone learns on initiation.'

Another buzz. Not until the boy had sat down did it cease.

'What is it you call the masquerade leaf?' Joseph asked. 'I've heard that nonsense a number of times, since I came to Nade.'

Many in the class looked from one to another con-

116

spiratorially, then at the teacher. Nobody would dare disclose the secret. They could not even disclose that the leaf was not botanical but just the names of two insignificant creatures which represent the sign of the cult. (The Nigerian Society for Preservation of African Culture forbids that the names be revealed.) 'Just as only the secretive herbalist knows which particular shrub in the vast forest can do the work, so also only the initiated should know which two creatures in the vast animal world represent the sign of the cult.' That was one of the laws every initiate learnt amidst the ritualistic torture of his initiation. The strokes which they had on their backs at that terrible moment had left big mental scars, an ingrained complex about the cult, in them for life.

'Stand up now and say it,' Joseph demanded.

The boy stood up and said, his voice shaking in feigned nervousness: 'It's iroko leaf.'

'Are you telling the truth?'

'It's true, sah,' confirmed the initiated among the boys, seriously. That was a trick each of them had learnt at initiation, to mention any ordinary leaf in times of difficulty. It did not matter if eventually the inquisitive stranger or uninitiate discovered that there was a different leaf each time. Some discovery would only deepen the mystery about the cult.

Indeed, Joseph was completely deceived. The customs of the tribesmen, though the same in essence, are often so different in the local expressions that what obtains in one clan area does not necessarily obtain among the neighbours. In Okpa which was his home town, the cult had a password; there was nothing like masquerade leaf. He dismissed the whole thing as extremely foolish and went off to say some very unfriendly things about pagans, masquerades and idols, after which he announced:

'We will go into town this morning to bring back some of the absentees.'

'We are afraid, Master,' replied Azuka on behalf of the class.

'You are afraid of what?'

'Masquerades will flog us, Master.'

Joseph deliberated within himself. He decided to put out a feeler more powerful than any before.

'And you call yourselves Christians? Those things which

117

you see are bad men, pagans in dirty masks and crests. Why fear them?'

They reacted instantaneously. Some shrugged; some even held their ears in horror. Such things must never be said with the mouth or heard with the ears. That was one more of the unforgettable laws learnt during initiation. 'Will you with your mouth, you child, disclose a spirit?' the tall and terrible flagellant of a masquerade had asked while exploding its cane on the candidate's back. 'Say not even in the grave.' Shaking and shrinking, the candidate repeated: 'Not even in the grave.' Then the masquerade picked up a double-edged knife and brushed it determinedly on a whetting stone. A constellation of sparks shone and went off. It bore down on the candidate, thundering in the secret chamber: 'I'll cleave your head into two unless your promise to tell me, as soon as you've been taught that, what moves inside mask.' No, never; not even in the grave! the candidate replied. Let the head go off instead! At which, the masquerade dropped the knife and picked up the cane again. . . . They still remembered the ordeal and the circumstances in which they made the vow.

Joseph observed the troubled expression on their faces. Truly, these people's reverence for masked bodies was congenital, he told himself. The time was not ripe yet to tackle them on the cult. He would do that some day; in the meantime, he must beat a retreat.

'All right then, forget all about masquerades and let's talk about something else,' he said. 'If you can't go into town to bring them today, we'll go after the celebrations.'

'Yes, Master,' they all accepted enthusiastically. It was the type of adventure they liked very much, especially as for some time now they had not had that.

'Next Friday then. Will the festival be over by then?'

'Yes, Master.'

'Unless of course they are all back by then. But don't tell them.'

'Yes, Master.'

Five pupils were still absent on Friday. Of the five, one was to Joseph the most important. He was Imo, one of the paramount chief's many sons. Imo was the first son of his mother who was clearly the least dear to her husband of the seven wives he had. The view was held among his paternal aunts that he had joined Joseph's gang on the prompting of his mother, nicknamed Husband's Bane.

'Other's could wait,' Joseph said after morning assembly. 'We'll go out now to bring Imo back. Let's make an example of a chief's son.'

Soon they were all lined up, in a single file with Joseph at the rear, wearing a white helmet on his head. They set out, silent at first, but later broke into a song which was succeeded by a prayer.

Nade went astir. People wondered who was the target. Frantically, women called in their small children and the men kept guard, gallantly, in the forehouses. Those who actually met the procession murmured a curse or an abuse, then prayed that the villains would keep moving and not stop anywhere in the neighbourhood. None dared to disturb, however.

Midway to the destination, Joseph halted them.

'Scatter now and meet there from different directions.' He pulled up his sagging hose. 'Four groups.' He cut the line into four and appointed the leaders, or whom Nnanna was one. 'Any group to get there first should go in from the back.'

Chief Eke had planned his palace in such a way that all his wives lived close to the rear compound wall; and each of the houses, which in fact were only huts, had an emergency exit leading outside the palace. Noiselessly, the first group arrived. They found the door barred. They began to debate in whispers who should kick first. Then the second group arrived, noiselessly too.

It was this second group that Nnanna led. 'What is the difficulty?' Nnanna inquired impatiently. Pushing the cowards aside, he kicked. He kicked again.

'Who is that mad villain?' shouted a woman's angry voice from within. Before the mad villain could reply she added: 'May your feet turn to ashes!'

Nnanna whispered something. They lifted him up. With both his hands he swept away the palm-frond stalks that covered the top of the wall. Then he went over the wall and dropped inside.

Imo was in the house with his mother. They had each a hoe

in hand ready to return to the farm after a break for breakfast. Imo at once realized what was on. He made to run away. But Nnanna dashed after him, caught him before he could take four paces and held him firmly. Imo struggled to free himself but Nnanna brought him down on the ground and held him there. He was definitely younger than his captor and was no match for him.

All this time Imo's mother had been watching them in silence. At first she was merely startled at this strange visitation that scaled compound walls. Her heart was aflame when she now saw Imo, her own blood, struggling desperately to free himself. She rushed forward and lifted the hoe to strike Nnanna's head with the curved end. But as the weapon was descending, Nnanna kicked her hand with his left foot. It dropped.

She picked up the weapon again, but with her left. She struck furiously, aimlessly.

Nnanna screamed.

Some boys were already dropping down from the wall. They went straight to his rescue, in time to avert a concerted attack by mother and son. Next, they removed the bar on the door. The rest poured in.

In the meantime, Joseph had walked into the palace through the big double-folding gate and was now engaged in a battle of words with three of Eke's wives. These women had called him all sorts of names and he could no longer restrain himself.

'. . . An abominable creature like you!'

'Satan's daughter!' He removed the helmet on his head, for no reason, and the woman ducked.

'You are a pig in body and spirit,' another said.

'You are all as filthy as the juju doctors who bleed you to death,' he replied.

Another challenged him to deny that he came from Ossa, the land of strange habits, and to state why at his age he had no wife.

'I will tell you,' said he in Ibo, then completed in English: 'Provided you destroy your idols and come to church.'

'What have you just said, you wicked one?' protested the woman . . .

A fairly large crowd had been drawn to this noisy scene.

Someone among them gave a cry of surprise and directed attention to the group that was coming up from behind.

'Who did it?' Joseph shouted to the boys, shaking his head commendatorily.

'Master, it's Nnanna,' answered many voices. Ibe added: 'his mother nearly crushed Nnanna's head. She got him on the hand.'

'Let me see.'

Nnanna came forward and showed the hand.

'Does it pain you much?'

'No, Master,' he replied.

Joseph rubbed hard on the injured knuckles with his palm. 'I'll smear it with ointment when we return,' said he. Then he demanded: 'Where is the one who lifted a weapon against a schoolboy? If she were a man she would be sentenced to jail for as many years as there are grains on a big cob of maize. Let her do it again and she will be made to suffer like a man.'

A murmur of abuse.

'We've come to take our members back to the school. We only wish we had found the chief himself in.'

They called him a kidnapper.

'Boys, what are you doing?'

'We are carrying him!'

'Carrying tru—'

' – ant,' they completed and swept Imo off the ground up to their heads, very impressively.

'Hee pee peep!'

'Ouraah!' Their voices rang in the neighbourhood like the echo of a big explosion.

As they began to leave, the crowd broke out into further abuse. Some called Joseph a beast; some called him a pestilence as horrible as the great artist. They were at least free to exercise their tongue, declared the women of the palace, and with that they went off cursing with the bitterest hate they could muster in their hearts. Imo's mother, now recovering her power of speech, asked her dead father's spirit to strangle Nnanna within a week and spare nobody who might contemplate his funeral obsequies. But Joseph advised his boys to ignore the babble of pagans.

Back to the school, Joseph made a fairly long speech in which he sentenced Imo to a term of three months in his house. During that period Imo would not be permitted to step outside the premises. Then he lauded their efficiency in apprehending the truant. For Nnanna Okafo he had special words of praise which he would not utter yet, he added. Then he concluded mercifully:

'It's already past noon and there's not much time left. We shall do only English and Religion, after which you can all go home.'

On the small and scaly blackboard he wrote out six alliterative words. Opposite each word he wrote the vernacular. Then he picked up his stick and pointed at the first word.

'Lion, all of you.'

Most of them said 'Tzaion'. Nade belongs to that small but influential minority of the tribe who find it very hard to reconcile their tongues to the sound of the letter o.

'Not tza—' he objected. 'Say, la—'

'Tra—'

'Lion!' he cried impatiently.

'Traion,' they conceded.

'Disappointing!' said Joseph to himself, then: 'Lion is agu.'

They echoed.

'Again.'

They repeated.

'Again.'

They repeated.

'Let somebody speak English with "lion".'

Hands went up.

'Ibe.'

'Nnanna Okafo, he is a tzaion,' Ibe said.

Even Ibe had already relapsed! exclaimed Joseph. However, he admitted to himself, the sentence was excellent. He took the opportunity to release a few of the special words of praise he had reserved for Nnanna.

NINETEEN

There were in the house when Nnanna returned from school that afternoon, his mother, Oji and two others. One of the two was a middle-aged man who was blind in one eye; his name was Okere. The other, a woman, Nnanna easily identified as Imo's mother. The atmosphere in the house was by no means friendly. The women were exchanging words and the men were doing their impartial best to keep them quiet.

'Here he comes!' Imo's mother broke out fitfully. 'That's the villain who climbed into my yard to attack me and my son. Come on now and complete it here. I'm sure it was your mother who sent you.'

'You two, do you hear the nonsense that comes out of her mouth!' Chiaku protested.

Once more the men intervened. Oji advised Chiaku to keep her mouth sealed. Okere ruled that it was unfair to blame the boy's mother. To which, Imo's mother replied:

'Is it fair then that he should jump into my house to attack me and my child? Who in this world would tolerate such treatment? And yet my fellow-woman talks to me the way she does!'

'It's enough now, woman,' Chiaku answered. 'Go back to your house and don't come here again to annoy me. Perhaps you want to show me that your husband is a chief.'

'I know you are terribly unhappy about that,' Imo's mother said boastfully.

'Very. Especially as, of all his wives, he loves you most!'

'Shut up, Chiaku!' Oji intervened again. 'You women always behave like small children. I'm sure you would resort to your claws and teeth if we left you alone.' To the other: 'I can understand your feeling; what he did is very bad indeed.'

'Your mouth will keep you long,' she promptly acknowledged.

'But then, it isn't on Chiaku that you should vent your anger. She's as innocent as you and I and Okere here.'

'Chief's wife indeed!' Chiaku sneered. 'How many times has

your husband talked to you this year, or accepted a meal from you?'

Imo's mother shook her head and bit her lower lip and sighed bitterly. 'Thunder will strike you dead one of these days,' she swore, pointing at Nnanna. 'Evil thing! As for the abuse I've received from your mother this afternoon, let me go home first and think.'

'Yes, go home straight and think yourself to death,' Chiaku said.

'You will see.'

Silent, they watched her leave.

'You know, I don't blame her much,' Oji said. 'My sister, you shouldn't have spoken to her the way you did.'

'She has good cause to be angry – if what she said is true,' Okere concurred.

'Of course it is. Why did you climb over the wall, Nnanna?' Oji asked.

'We went in a group to take Imo to the school,' Nnanna replied complacently.

'And of the whole accursed gang you were the only one they could select to somersault over the wall?' asked Chiaku in anger. 'I am not enough for you; you want to carry your iniquity to others too.'

'If she comes here again I will return her curse regardless of her age.'

'Keep your mouth closed. It's you who fouled the air we breathe.'

'Never you climb walls again, my son,' Okere said with humour. 'They may begin to think that you are practising for burglary.'

Oji laughed. Nnanna smiled. Chiaku sobbed.

Okere rose. 'I had better go home now. I'll come tomorrow morning to cut down the palm fruit for you, Chiaku.'

'Please don't forget.'

He began to leave. She fixed her eyes on him and she contemplated the big and hairy thigh muscles, the sturdy build and a head beautifully flattened at the top – features which made him convincingly masculine. The sight gave Chiaku a deep pleasure. It re-kindled a longing which for years she had successfully stifled.

Fifteen years, or more, it was now. She had resolved not to marry again. Not that custom forbade a widow to re-marry: but it was far more honourable for a woman, once widowed, and provided she had a male child who would continue the lineage, to remain a widow. There could be no greater service to the late husband than to stay with the son and thus remain the custodian of the lineage, until such a time as that son would grow up into a man. All these years Chiaku had faced, or suffered, with determination the logic of the resolution – she had kept her body away from men. And the more the child grew up and gave promise of success, the less painful did she find that logic, until the longing was almost extinct in her.

Of late however it had revived in her, this longing. But it came in mild and occasional tugs. This afternoon it was both sustained and intense.

Suddenly she turned away her face. She must not let her eyes betray her feeling – not even to her own brother. No good woman would. She said, shouting so that Okere could hear:

'There are three or four palm-trees I would like you to trim for me when you come tomorrow.'

'All right.' He was already at the door.

Oji too left soon after.

Then Nnanna went to the kitchen wall to remove his lunch. He found the niche empty. He returned to the parlour with a heavy face.

'Is there nothing for me to eat?'

'They didn't cook for you there?' she asked in reply.

'Who?'

'Those that selected you to climb the wall for them.'

He collapsed on the floor. He faced her with a look so anguished as to compel compassion. Relenting, she explained:

'I've not cooked yet. I was afraid you would reject it as you did yesterday, when you accused me of putting some festive meal into your lunch.'

He blinked away the explanation, pouting. She observed him furtively. He would soon rise and begin to fling things out, said she in her mind. That was the way he reacted to extreme hunger. He had a stomach that tormented when it was empty. Like his late father. Or even Amanze. It was a family trait. They hurled expletives and objects at you if you starved them.

'Let me go and put some slices of yam on the fire for you.'
She left for the kitchen.

The ointment which the teacher rubbed on Nnanna's injured knuckles after school seemed to have had no noticeable effect. In fact, the pain had continued to increase since then. From time to time on his way home, Nnanna had exposed the hand to the sun so that the thing would melt right into the skin and kill the pain.

The noisy scene he met in the house had some anaesthetic effect on him. Now that the place was quiet, he began to feel the pain again. He examined the hand; he found that it had grown bigger. To add to that, he now felt some burning pain, and a weight up in his shoulder.

Soon, the heat superseded the original pain. He twisted and stretched; he hissed.

Then it seemed as if he had the hand in an invisible fire.

'Mother!' he cried, twice.

'What?'

'My hand!'

'Did what?'

'Come and see.'

She came. She examined the hand. 'What happened to it?'

'It's the spot where she hit me with her hoe.'

'Who?' she demanded indignantly.

'Imo's mother.' He hissed again.

'May a falling tree knock her down dead! She did this to you and yet she had the courage to come here and bark like a mad dog. I'll find some oil for it. Or what have you got on it already?'

'It's something the teacher rubbed in at the school.'

She winked deprecatingly and turned away her face.

She went and brought some linseed oil from the middle room. She rubbed, superimposing it on the ointment. He gave an agonized cry.

'You have refused to hear with your ears!' said she in rebuke. 'That place will be your end if you don't take time.'

She returned to the kitchen. But not long after, he summoned her again. She came hastily.

This time she found him writhing on the floor and blowing at the hand at short intervals.

'It burns worse than fire now!' he cried.

'Isn't it just the swelling?' She examined the hand again. 'Hei-i-i!' It was becoming turgid.

'Bring water and pour on it!'

She brought a cup of water. She poured it on the swelling. He found it soothing. But only for a minute or so. The pain started again, growing steadily until it almost exceeded its former intensity. He cried and groaned.

'What is it, Nnanna?' asked she with trepidation. 'Have you been poisoned?'

He blew at the hand.

'I had better go and see Oji.'

She went out hurriedly and returned hurriedly. Shortly after, Oji came. An amateur doctor, Oji examined the hand carefully.

'Don't touch it again,' said he, very composed. 'Let me go and find something in the bush to check the pain. The swelling will certainly go down when the pain has ceased.'

'Look at your sister!' Chiaku exclaimed.

'Keep quiet. It's nothing.'

'Let it be nothing!' she grumbled to herself. 'I know there's nothing that matters to you.'

She sat down close by Nnanna, as if guarding him against Death. This was a situation to which she was quite unused. He was hardly ever ill. Only twice had she had cause to get worried about his health. The first time was when he was only two years old. He had a very high temperature then; his breathing was not free; he was bony and weak and his eyes were pale. The other was eight years back. She had never understood what was wrong with him on that occasion, but she would always remember a particular day when the sick child on her lap went stiff and she addressed in song the almost lifeless body: 'Nnadim, what is it you want to do to me . . .?' A few minutes later, his limbs moved and his jaws unlocked into a feeble cry. Since then, Nnanna had not been really sick. It was the case with all healthy people: they paid their arrears whenever sickness got real hold of them.

'You said something was rubbed on it at that place?' she asked reflectively.

'Yes.'

'Couldn't that be the cause?'

'No.'

'Did a masquerade flog you recently?'

'No.'

'Or touch you?'

'No.'

'Or give you a chase?'

'No?'

'Or look at you steadily for a period of time?'

He shouted: 'No. Don't ask me those questions again!'

She picked up a small mat tray. With that he began to fan the hand. He asked her to fan harder, which she did, until she began to perspire.

Nearly twenty minutes passed.

'I think it's beginning to lessen.'

'May it be true.' She continued to fan.

Oji returned with some tender roots and green leaves. He crushed them together on a grinding stone, then gathered the pieces into his right palm. Over Nnanna's swollen knuckles he pressed the effect hard until the medicinal drips had touched most of the surface. Finally, he knocked his fist together.

'That thing you've just done is not good,' Nnanna objected, looking seriously annoyed.

'What nonsense is he talking?' Chiaku asked.

'Bring an egg, Chiaku. Quick!' Oji said, ignoring the protest altogether.

'What do you want it for?' demanded Nnanna.

'Don't waste time!' he urged.

She went and brought an egg. She gave it to him. He knocked at the shell with the tip of his middle finger, until it was broken.

'Bring the hand.'

'No!' Nnanna refused and shook his head stoutly.

'Go on!' Chiaku intervened. 'Give him your hand, you lunatic creature.'

'I will not,' said Nnanna firmly, and he stood up as if in readiness for an encounter. 'I will not let you people spill an egg on me.'

'Why?' Oji asked.

'It is sin.' He stepped sideways, away from them.

'You would rather die?'

'Yes; let me die instead,' replied he with the spirit of a

martyr. 'You might as well go and bring a dibia with painted eyelids.'

There was tense silence.

'It's now clear that something terrible has happened to your head,' Chiaku said. 'You are more mad than Uche of Umudiobia who sleeps on treetops.'

'Let it be. You people do all sorts of things in the name of medicine.'

'Villain!'

'I accept I am. And that's why you mask human beings and call them spirits!' He grinned.

Oji's big frame shook and he gave a deep, thoughtful groan. Then he threw out the broken egg and wiped his hands dry. Chiaku was utterly confused. She spat and she snapped her fingers. She said:

'Your death becomes imminent the moment such things begin to come out of your mouth. That decides it anyway: I shall soon leave this house to you alone.'

'What about my lunch?' he asked, grinning.

This infuriated her all the more and compelled Oji to speak:

'You are completely lost now, my son.'

TWENTY

'I want to tell you something,' she said. 'I've been meaning to do so for a long time now.' That was months later. She was eating her supper.

'Yes?' he said.

She threw out a lump. It fell at the usual place. 'To you I fly, Igwe!' she prayed. 'You who own heaven and earth.' She threw again.

'Is that the thing you want to tell me?'

'May your mouth be sealed,' she answered him. 'You take delight in making fun of the mother who bore you in her womb.'

'My mouth is sealed now.' He tapped at his lips. 'Throw away the whole food if you like; I won't talk again. It's your own share after all.'

She ate on without further interruption. About to finish, she spoke again:

'If you care to listen, may I tell you the thing now?'

'I'm listening,' he replied.

She hesitated. 'You are my son,' she began. The tone was calm and the mood was friendly. 'I carried you inside my womb for ten moons not less a day. In addition, you are my husband's father come to life.' She licked her fingers dry of soup and put the pot aside. In the brief interval of time, she organized her mind. 'There's therefore nothing I should hide from you. 'Nothing at all, even though you treated me the way you did. That's why I decided to tell you. It doesn't matter whether you like it or not, for who would allow herself to live as I do if she had a chance?'

'What is it again?' asked he, rather intrigued at the circumlocution.

She took no notice of the question. 'I've no money left. It all went into you. There's only one goat in the shed now; the rest are either dead or sold. The poultry has been cleared by disease. How then can I remain here?' She paused. 'I didn't want to tell you until I was sure. Or perhaps you know already.'

'Know what?'

'Well, if you don't know, I've decided to marry.'

'To do what?'

She tried to browbeat. She said in an offended tone: 'I say I've decided to marry. I will then leave this house for you and your friends. You are an adult now, almost; and you are fearless and strong. You should be able to look after yourself.'

'You will leave me here alone?'

'Yes,' she said firmly.

They gazed at each other in silence.

'Where will you go?'

'You mean who is he?'

'Yes,' said he in an alienated tone.

'You know him.' Her voice sank. She said uneasily: 'He is Okere, the one you've been seeing here.'

He began to understand. Of late the man Okere had been

130

visiting the house at all hours. Once, recently, he had surprised him talking right into her ear. A wild impulse had come into him then and he nearly challenged the one-eyed short man to state what business he had in the house which should be bringing him there at all hours and giving him access to every corner. But she, reading his mind, tried to explain. Okere had been helping her a great deal of late, she said. And so on, and so on. Of course he did not stay to listen; he left them there and went to see Ibe . . .

'Is that why he has been coming here?'

Her silence confirmed.

'You can't wait?'

'What for? Today is as good as tomorrow, my son.'

He turned away his face. 'I'll continue to go to school if that is your reason,' he whined. 'You can go to any place you like.'

'I knew that's what you would say.' Her voice descended. 'It's not only that anyway. Your mother is already delicate. I'm sure you know what I mean.'

'I know nothing,' he answered sharply.

'Turn round and listen to me, Nnanna,' she pleaded. 'I must tell you everything plainly. Go on, turn round and don't turn your back to your mother like that.' He still would not turn. 'Well, let me say it out, whether you are listening or not: I am two bodies.'

He was terribly exacerbated. 'Don't tell me anything again,' he said. 'If you leave I too will go away. I can't stay here alone.'

She lowered her head. How could she expect him to stay alone in the house, in those surroundings? Especially during the nights when darkness filled everywhere and the owl hooted and insects shrilled and spirits roamed! In dream he would be tormented by things that flew in the air as well as by those that crept on the surface of the earth; waking, he would find himself alone and helpless, buried deep in boundless darkness. That was too much for any child of his age. He was still a yam sapling; he still required tending. But then, it was too late to reconsider things. She had taken the final decision. 'That decides it for me. . . .' She had meant those words. It was almost three moons now; the child in her womb was nearly three moons already, though one could hardly notice that, for she was of the small-womb type.

'Why don't you come and stay there with me?' she suggested absurdly.

'Never!' He sprang up from the floor.

'Stay with Oji then.'

'No. I must go away!' He entered the middle room.

'Go where?'

'To any place at all, but I must leave here.' There was in his tone that ring of sad determination which warned her whenever his will had become inflexible.

Later that night, as Nnanna lay awake wondering where he could go, a recollection came to his mind. The week before, Joseph had told them something about the new priest who lived at Ossa on a hill. The priest had just come from Ahia to start the new Ossa parish which included Nade and all the towns around. He would visit Nade in four weeks' time and was anxious to take with him on his return to Ossa any two good boys who were willing to follow.

A lot of strange stories had been told about small and distant Ossa spread on a hill. The soil was arid – so much that the inhabitants bought most of their food. There was only one tiny spring to serve the entire population, and this was dry for the greater part of the year; fortunately, however, the townsmen relished brown flood water and even preferred it to spring water. Then there were such social curiosities like the young breaking kolanut for the old; or the women tilling the soil faster than the men; or the men slicing boiled cassava better than the women. Some of the stories were blatantly untrue, yet no less popular. Like the one about poison-brewing being the people's main occupation. Or that which said that all the evil spirits in the world met there at the end of every moon to plan their strategy against men. But the most popular was the one about the aged savouring the liver of adolescents.

Such stories, whether true or false, had automatically eliminated Ossa from the list of places worth visiting, so that when Joseph made the announcement, not one boy in the school received it with enthusiasm. Not even the additional information that Ossa was quite a short distance from Okpa, the teacher's home-town, would move them. Some declined outright, shrugging. Some whispered that they would not allow toothless jaws to munch their liver. Nnanna was one of those who had made a joke of the idea.

Necessity now forced Nnanna's mind open. He wondered if Ossa could be as bad as that, when both the priest and the District Commissioner lived there. The Commissioner had, so the teacher had said, soldiers and policemen who were armed to the teeth and who could destroy any town, no matter the size, in a single day. Where else could life be secure if not in such a place?

He decided that he would volunteer. And with that, Nnanna felt that release of mind, sudden and complete, which comes to one who has just discovered the only possible solution to a puzzle. He resolved too to seal his mind against any further ideas.

Not long after, he fell asleep. But it was as yet a shallow sleep punctuated with snappy, discomforting dreams, mostly about Ossa on a hill. Not until the first cockcrow did he sink deep. By the time he woke, the sun was already sending tiny rods of light into the room through the leaks in the thatch roof.

Hastily, he rose and went outside. He looked round. It seemed the morning was already advanced. Then, as he was still trying to gauge the time from the brightness of the atmosphere, he heard the school bell pealing the frantic dactyls that gave the seven o'clock warning. He went in and began to prepare.

He managed to reach the school before the second bell. For most of the day he watched out for a quiet opportunity to speak to the teacher. It did not come – not until at the close of school. As the pupils, now discharged from order, were shouting homewards, he went up to Joseph and said:

'Master, there's something I wish to tell you.'

'Is it something important?' asked Joseph.

'Yes, Master.'

'Follow me to the house then.'

'Yes, Master.'

In the house, he stood a respectful distance from the teacher.

'Yes, what is it?' indicated Joseph from his easy chair, handkerchief in hand.

'Master, I want to leave our house.'

'To leave your house?'

'Yes, Master.'

'Why?'

'My mother wants to go away, Master, and there will be nobody to stay there with me.'

'Where does she want to go?'

'She's going to marry, Master.'

'And leave you alone in the house!' he wondered aloud.

'Yes, Master.'

'Where do you want to go yourself?'

Nnanna hesitated. 'I don't know yet, Master. You told us something last week about the Reverend Father who will visit here soon.'

'Yes. And what about it?'

'Master, I would like to follow him.'

'You want to go to Ossa?'

'Yes, Master, if you select me.'

'I see,' grunted Joseph thoughtfully. He wiped his face with the handkerchief. After that, he began to twirl the cloth before him. For the afternoon was hot – so hot that the air simmered. He said: 'Do you think you can live there?'

'Yes, Master,' Nnanna replied promptly.

'When will your mother leave?'

'Master, she hasn't said yet, but I know it will be soon.'

He gathered the handkerchief into a ball and inserted it under his left armpit.

'All right; I've heard you. Today is what?'

'Wednesday, Master.'

'See me again on Friday about it, before school begins.'

'Yes, Master.'

'I'll tell you my decision then. You can go home now.'

Nnanna left the house. He went to see Ibe.

On Friday, he arrived at the school much earlier than usual and made straight for the teacher's house.

'Master, you told me to see you today,' he said.

'Oh yes, I've not forgotten,' Joseph replied. 'It's about Ossa, isn't it?'

'Yes, Master.'

'Do you still want to go?'

'Yes, Master.'

'Right. I'll speak to Father when he comes.'

'Yes, Master.' He almost exclaimed.

'You don't know yet when your mother will leave?'

'No, Master.'

'If she leaves before then, you can come over here and stay.'

'Yes, Master. Thank sah, Master.'

Joseph got him to tidy up his language before he could leave the house.

TWENTY-ONE

Then he watched to see if she was packing her things. Every day he would ask her if she still wanted to go away. She would reply that she was sure to leave, and that soon, but when exactly she had not decided. Yet, unknown to him, she had been removing her things in small and unnoticeable quantities to her new home.

One day he returned from school to find that she was not in the house, and was not anywhere in the immediate neighbourhood. He went to the usual niche, removed his lunch and sat down to eat. When he touched the food his face clouded and he sighed disgustedly. The yam was cold. He had asked her – many, many times! – not to keep him cold meals which froze the intestines.

For some time he regarded both the food and the container with extreme malevolence. Then he began to eat. He ate hurriedly. They had a Spelling Match in the school that afternoon and he was anxious to get there in time. He would be paired with Ibe against two other friends. The losing side would be liable to a fine of coconut and toasted maize, to be paid within four days. It was a new idea, the Spelling Match. It was introduced by Joseph, though the details – the teams and the fine – were worked out by the pupils themselves.

He abandoned the meal midway and went out to the front-yard to gauge the time. He was at once struck by the density of the silence around. It seemed as if desolation had already crept into the place. Not even from the goat-shed would a single sound come, which was surprising. Open Mouth could not keep its mouth shut within a count of twenty-one, hence Oji gave it that name.

He went to the shed to see. The goat was not there. And the whole length of the tether was gone too. It could not have broken loose then, he reasoned. Somebody must have removed it. A thief? He had better go in and see. Perhaps there were some other things missing beside the animal.

Nnanna went into the middle room. He looked round; then up at the wall rack. Yes, something was missing. What was it? The long basket in which she took things to market! That day was? Afo. Could she have gone to Afoibe, the distant eight-day market where livestock sold dearest, of all known markets? But she couldn't have – not when she was in up to the time he left for school. 'He that goes to Afoibe must set out earlier than the sun.' Perhaps Oji knew something about it.

He went to see Oji.

He found Oji in the forehouse diligently padding his climbing rope.

'Do you know where Mother is?'

'No,' Oji replied. 'Why do you ask?'

'Our goat is missing.'

'Missing?' asked he after a momentary pause.

'It is not in the shed and there is no sign of the tether.'

'Could it have been removed by a thief?'

'I don't know. And Mother's market basket is not there either.'

'It's beginning to sound more strange. Any other things?'

'I only noticed the goat and the basket.'

Oji stopped what he was doing and fed his nostrils. 'It's strange indeed,' he said, nasally, his thumb-nail ready with one more helping. 'But I don't think it's the work of thieves. We have never had thieves in our quarter. Let's wait till your mother returns. You had better go back and look after the house.'

'I'm going to some other place.'

He emptied the snuff into his nostril. He cried 'A-a-ah!' and blew his nose. 'Well,' said he, 'when you are both back in the evening we shall be able to know what has happened.'

A very thin film of daylight was all that remained when

Nnanna returned in the evening. In the open yard Chiaku was sitting on a dwarf stool, silent and motionless. The background of an imperfect darkness imbued her figure with a transitory, ghostly quality.

'Who is that?' he demanded.

'I,' she said. 'Nnanna?'

'Yes!'

'Just returning?' she queried.

He had come closer. 'I was frightened.'

'Why?'

'I couldn't quite say what I thought you were.'

'A big boy like you?'

'Is it long since you returned?'

'Not very. Did you find the lunch I kept for you?'

'Yes,' he said coldly. 'How does one enter the house?'

'Go in and make fire.'

'You left it until I would return?'

'I'm not staying,' Chiaku said. 'I've only come to see you and will soon go back.'

'Go where?'

'To his house – I mean Okere's.'

There was an interval of time.

'So you are now ready to move?'

'Well, yes,' she stammered. 'But not completely; I shall come back tomorrow to see you.'

'Thank you!' He spoke indignantly. 'I will stay here for you to come and see me!'

'I mean to be coming, my son,' she pleaded. 'But if you are afraid and will not come with me either, why not go and stay in Oji's house at least for the night?'

'I won't,' said he with finality, his voice rising. 'And don't you come here to look for me. Immediately you step out now I too will leave.'

'Leave for where?'

'Anywhere I like.' His eyes had filmed. Big drops of tears came down. But she could not see them – so dim was the light now. She only noticed that his voice quavered. 'I know now, it was you who removed the goat and the basket.'

'Don't cry, my husband's father,' she pleaded. 'Why not come with me for this night at least?'

Silent with anger, Nnanna walked into the dark house. Having groped for some minutes, he came out bringing in his two hands those things he belied Joseph would tolerate – his small pants, yellow singlet, loin cloth and the small wooden board of crude workmanship which he used in school.

'Leave now,' he challenged, 'and see if I too won't leave.'

She laughed mirthlessly. 'Chiaku has no more energy left in her to think about you.' Then she rose and began to leave. In spite of those words, she went out with a worried mind.

A few yards from the entrance door, Chiaku halted and looked back. She emitted a sigh. He was coming; he was close behind. Confusion!

She turned and continued, without saying a single word. On and on Nnanna followed. It seemed as if he was going to Okere's house with her. Then they came to a big road fork. There he turned off and took the direction of the school.

TWENTY-TWO

She found Okere smooth-tempered and easy to please. He was not a particularly handsome man – his face was freckled and his nose was flat and he was blind in one eye; but his striking masculinity amply atoned for everything. Though twice widowed and a father of four, he looked an altogether eligible bachelor, from the physical point of view. Then there was the fact that he was of the same parents as Ego's mother. By an odd turn of events, they were still in-laws – Chiaku and Ego's mother, only that the direction was reversed.

There was a common saying that a new wife, if she be sensible, should first seek to know the extent of her husband's land and the fruit trees thereon. Chiaku did. What she saw confirmed her hopes. Okere belonged to a family which in every respect was obi. Uka, his father, had been a very big landowner, a wealthy farmer and a husband of five. When he died his land was partitioned between the five houses in the

138

family, and it was left to the males of each mother to sub-divide their own share as equitably as possible. Okere was the only son of his mother who was the first wife. The two facts combined gave him alone almost one-third of the family land, much to the jealousy of his fourteen half-brothers and the joy of his four sisters of whom Ego's mother was the eldest.

Chiaku certainly had plenty of land on which to farm. She had fruit trees too. Most important of all, she was two bodies already and the child seemed to be developing well. Who knew if it would be a boy! she would tell herself. Perhaps her chi was going to be sympathetic here – at long last! But she must not conclude yet. Did she not start well enough in Umudiobia? Or in Nade, when she returned? She should keep open the palm of her hand and receive with resignation whatever would be de-livered into it. It was quite possible, for example, that Okere's brothers would start something over his share of the family land. And then, there were all sorts of gossips and indelicacies going on among their wives and sisters. One of them had quipped that Okere's excessive virility would always leave him a widower. Another had attributed his loss of one eye to some concealed crime and gone on to remark that only the most fool-hardy would accept him for a husband.

She must keep out of such vicious talk, she resolved. She would behave like a sensible woman, one who had learnt her lesson in life. 'When a woman trips and falls the second time you can enumerate all she has inside the basket on her head.' She had abandoned two homes; she had laid bare her inner self.

Above all, she must make a special effort to satisfy her hus-band, bearing in mind that she was not a brand-new acqui-sition, or a depth yet to be fathomed. What was it people said in proverb? A trap would snap and catch if the prey should come for the bait the third time. Proverbs are food for the wise.

From time to time, Chiaku's mind went back to her son who now lived with a stranger. Each time her conscience stung her, reminding her that a child was a child, no matter what his offence. She found it impossible to remove Nnanna's image from her mind or to regard him as lost when he was not only alive but also within reach. One day she decided to go and see him.

It was exactly twenty days since their parting. She left after lunch. Near the mission premises she turned off and went to the back of the teacher's residence. Keeping a safe distance from the edge of the compound, she called.

'Who is that?' Nnanna answered.

'Is that Nnanna?'

'Yes. Who are you?'

'It's I, your mother.'

'Where are you?'

'Behind, outside the premises. Come here and take a message.'

A few minutes later they stood facing each other. He regarded with sharp unbelieving eyes. She was much changed. The bulge of pregnancy, now manifest, had destroyed her erect and regular figure. Her face was pale, shrivelled and dry.

'I've come to see you,' she said, anxious to divert his attention from her appearance.

'Let's go to the house.'

She waved eloquently. 'I've brought you some sliced cassava. I hope you still eat it, or does the man also forbid you to taste such things?'

She brought out the packet from her bag. She gave it to him. Without wasting time, he bored into it with his right thumb. His mouth over the hole, he pressed the packet until he had got a reasonable quantity inside his mouth.

Presently Joseph's voice rang from the house.

'Sa-a-ah!' Nnanna answered. He sounded like a masquerade.

'From where do you answer?'

'I'm here, Master.' He swallowed hurriedly.

'Where?'

'Here, at the back of the house.'

'Terrible!' he exclaimed, then reverted into Ibo: 'You left the doors wide open and went out? What are you doing there?'

'I am with Mother, Master.'

'Did you say your mother?'

'Yes, Master.'

'Your own mother?'

'Yes, Master.'

Joseph paused. 'Why don't you bring her into the house?'

Nnanna tried again. She waved more forcefully than before.

'Master, she doesn't want to come in,' he reported.

140

'Tell her there's something important I want to talk to her about.'

He consulted. 'She says she will not come, Master, and that you had better come out here.'

Joseph took nearly a minute to make up his mind. 'Tell her to wait there; I am coming.'

He was out in a matter of minutes.

'Are you Nnanna's mother?' asked he with a tolerant smile on his face.

'I am,' Chiaku replied. Surprisingly, she appeared well-disposed.

'I've never met you before.'

'That's true.'

'As you can see for yourself, your son is all right.'

'I've already noticed that,' Chiaku acknowledged. 'He looks healthy and happy, for which I must thank you.'

'Your words are those of a sensible woman.'

'I only stated the fact. It's very kind of you, stranger that you are in our land, to take him on and look after him like your own brother.'

'In the Church we regard one another as brothers.'

No more of that type of talk! 'What was it you wanted to talk to me about?' she asked.

'Oh, yes,' said he in a casual manner. 'I want your son to follow the Father to Ossa.'

She stared at him with renewed interest. She said: 'I didn't understand what you said.'

'I intend to give Nnanna to the Reverend Father,' Joseph repeated, louder for emphasis.

'To whom?'

'To the white man who brought both the church and the school.'

'Why?' Her countenance turned hostile.

'He will take your son to Ossa on a hill, there to bring him up.'

Her mouth twisted to the left and her cheek creased. She was deliberating.

'What do you say you want to do with my son, stranger?'

'For the third time, is it? Listen again: Father will take your son to Ossa when he comes. He will be here in ten days' time.'

'You want to sell him to the man?'

'Who said—'

'I hear that man has no children,' she interrupted. 'Perhaps he wants other people's and you help him to kidnap them.'

Joseph laughed indulgently.

'Look, I'm not the one you should speak to,' she went on querulously. 'Go and tell the men; I'm only a woman, a stranger in their family.'

'I know nobody but you.' He spoke coolly yet firmly.

She turned round and began to leave, trailing: 'Go to Umudiobia where he was born. Go and see Amanaze, his father's next of kin. Leave Chiaku alone.'

'You'd better go and tell them yourself.' He shouted so that she could hear.

Chiaku halted. She turned, facing them. She pulled at her ears and she opened her eyes to their very limit. Then:

'I beg the two of you, leave me alone. I've no more energy left in me to think about you and Nnanna.'

'Don't shout, Mother,' Nnanna pleaded.

'Take him anywhere you like and allow Chiaku to have some peace.'

'Don't shout, woman!' Joseph ordered.

'May thunder strike you dead there, you wicked man!'

They did not hear this, for her voice was very low.

TWENTY-THREE

It was a long time now since the priest last visited Nade. The new Ossa parish had not been set up then; it was from Ania that he came. To the townsmen that last visit was memorable in a way. They still talked about 'the hungry-looking one who threw coins at people'. They meant Reverend Father Patrick Ryan, tall and lean. Father Ryan, out of sheer generosity, threw handfuls of pennies at the curious crowd that assembled on his arrival. But his motive was imperfectly appreciated by the other side. 'Look at this white ichneumon fly who throws his own charm at people!' they sneered. Some said: 'He thinks we are so wretchedly poor as to be bewitched with money!' Then they abandoned the coins and went away – to the great delight of smart young ones among the Christians. Ryan was still at Ania but he would not come this time. It was Father Smith, the new priest at Ossa, who was being expected.

The Christians assembled in the church compound about eight in the morning. They were over a hundred in number, all neatly dressed for the occasion. The more prosperous ones wore leather or canvas shoes, and the most sophisticated of the men wore hats and sunshades in addition. Not long after, they set out together for the point at which the priest and his entourage were expected to enter the town.

They had been there for hours. The sun was touching the zenith and the shadow was at the feet. They wondered whether the priest would still come on that day. Then they heard voices shouting in excitement. The noise grew louder and louder. They moved on to that direction.

From the next bend ahead, a party of travellers appeared. In the midst of the party they saw a white man. That was he! they exclaimed. Hats went off.

He was a young man, probably in his late twenties. He was tall and held himself erect. His broad handsome face beamed with smiles all the time. His khaki shirt and shorts were rumpled and his hair unkempt, but these did not detract from a strong, compelling personality. At home in Ireland people had said of John Michael Smith that he had the personality of an overpaid young company director. At Ossa the Christians called him the well-fed new priest, in contrast to Father Ryan, while the natives said he was a wealthy man. 'He looks,' said they, 'like one fed by many wives.' Even there on the spot, some of his hosts had already put their heads together and named him the most handsome of all white men ever seen in the area.

After the necessary introductions they all went straight to the mission.

Father Smith paced up and down the premises reading some prayers. It was evening. From time to time he would look up at the sky, at sunset clouds in their clumsy flux.

Bold crimson patches lay on a background of deep blue. Father Smith stood motionless and looked on, like one entranced. He watched the crimson dissolve into coral pink and the deep blue into grey. The contour kept on changing. One mass of smoke after another would race stupidly up, interrupt the view, rise to a gaunt pinnacle, and finally dissolve itself.

He wrenched his eyes from the sight and tried to concentrate on the book in his hands. But a few minutes later, he found himself contemplating the sky again. It was as if his senses had revolted from his will! Perhaps that was proper, Smith reflected: here was a sight in which the mind should meet the heart: it was nature's pure art made purer still by its remoteness from man's touch. And God was nature . . .

A big, bloodthirsty mosquito hummed over his right ear. He hit furiously. He missed the insect and struck his ear. He cursed aloud. A strong breeze suddenly came. A land of contrasts indeed! he told himself, and shook his head and smiled.

He looked up again. The sight had now become a shifting mountain range, glowing colours on a shining background. He gazed steadily and his heart absorbed the purity of the glow and riot of colours. What moved him most in this his first experience of real tropical sunset was the harmony of it all — the harmony in speed as well as of proportions. When Joseph came close to his side he did not know. It was only when he heard the loud 'Good evening, Father' that he came suddenly to life.

'How are you, Joseph?' he asked in response.

'Very well, Father,' answered Joseph. 'I've come to see how Father is and also to tell Father something.'

'Thanks, Joseph. What is it you want to tell me?'

'Father, there's a boy in my school I would like to show you.'

'To show me?' He twisted his voice in surprise.

'Yes, Father.'

'What for?' asked he curiously.

'Father, you remember you said that you wanted two boys from here?'

'I did?'

'Yes, Father. In the letter you sent.'

'Oh, that?' He smiled. 'I've already found the two boys I wanted, Joseph. It was a general request I sent to all the stations in the parish.'

Disappointment dulled Joseph's face.

'But tell me, how is the one you want to show me? Is he a good lad?'

'Very good, Father,' said he loquaciously. 'It was I who converted him and he is staying with me at the moment. He has lost his father and his mother left him some weeks ago. She is remarried now and there's nobody to look after him.'

'So he is in need of care?' summarized Father Smith.

'Yes, Father.'

'What exactly would you want me to do for him then?'

'I ask, Father, that you take him with you to Ossa,' he entreated.

'Take him?'

'If you can, Father.'

'I see.' His face wrinkled with thought. 'Is he a good boy?'

'He is very good, Father.'

'And promising?'

'Yes, Father, he promises he will stay if you take him.'

'Not that,' said the priest with an amused smile. 'I mean, whether he is likely to remain a good boy.'

'I am sure, Father.'

Another strong wind started. It swept the priest's soutane into a billow and caused the leaves of the book in his hand to flutter.

'You can go now, Joseph, and mention it again tomorrow morning,' he said. 'Let me go in and continue my mission.'

'Yes, Father.'

Alone once more, Father Smith gazed at the sky as before. He was thinking, but not about the sunset this time. A good boy, of the promising type! That phrase had recalled to his mind, with considerable nostalgia, the incident of a particular day in his years in the seminary. It was at a sociology seminar and the Father Superior was stressing the necessity for winning as many converts as possible in what he described as the first concentrated invasion of tropical Africa. 'In this our early phase,' the Superior expatiated in his slow and solemn voice, as of a prayer, with so many Christian denominations literally pouring into that pagan world, our first emphasis must be on statistical successes. We must bring the word of God to as many as possible at the same time. We want on our side the vast numbers who in Africa of the future will sustain the church with their numerical strength. Call it vote of the masses if you like. In pursuit of that objective, I'm afraid we've got to be impatient with the culture of the people. There just isn't the time to sort out first and label their customs as acceptable and unacceptable. To be ruthless in our method and yet successful in our aim, we must ensure that all along we present to the people good tangible evidence of the advantages of Christianity.'

'But,' seminarist John Michael Smith had asked, 'should not success always be judged by the degree to which we, or rather our converts, approached the true Christian ideal? I had always felt that he were a better missionary who made a few but thorough conversions than one who amassed numbers that would relapse into paganism at the first shock. I would rather concentrate more on the promising ones, Father, and set about making them real good Christians.'

'Your view is appreciated, John,' the Superior had answered, 'but only up to a point. Nobody says that we should stop at amassing numbers, if I may borrow that awful expression from you. What I say is that we've got to move very fast in the first phase. The task of achieving a deep, rational and permanent acceptance of the faith had better be left to a later stage. Certainly we realize the imperfections of the first phase.'

'I'm for the early Jesuits in this,' Smith had insisted.

'Jesuits? Concentrate on the notable few, or on good and promising lads, who will influence the rest for good! My good idealist, the way of the early Jesuits cannot be ours in this task. This is no counter-reformation; rather, we are on a virgin soil, very vast too, and we want acres and acres of it to ourselves. Besides, you can never be sure of your promising ones, human nature being what it is.'

Seeing the serious expression on the father Superior's face, Smith came to realize that he had exhausted the amount of freedom of speech permissible, even in a seminar. He sat down. But from that day the idea had stuck in his mind: It was better to train a few converts thoroughly in the first instance and use them as examples to convert their brothers than to spread a thin layer of the thing on vast numbers at the same time. This was his second month as a missionary in Africa, he now told himself; this could be his first chance of testing his conviction.

At mid-morning the following day, Joseph brought Nnanna before him. He regarded the boy, from the legs up to the trunk – healthy-looking, all symmetrical, the dark skin flushed with the freshness of adolescence. Father Smith tapped at Nnanna's cheeks, fondly. With that touch, a certain sensation, a mixture of pleasure and sympathy, went into him. He asked, looking right into the frightened eyes:

'You want to follow me to Ossa?'

Nnanna could not make out a single word. Joseph came to his rescue:

'Do you want to go to Ossa with Father?'

'I want,' Nnanna uttered.

'Say that in English,' said Father Smith.

'I going to the Ossa, Father.'

Joseph winked eloquently.

'You'll arrange to inform his people, Joseph,' said the priest, quite impressed at the effort.

'Yes, Father.' Immediately they began to move away, he ordered Nnanna to repeat the sentence about going to Ossa.

TWENTY-FOUR

Joseph regarded as a great achievement on his part the fact that Father Smith had agreed to take Nnanna away to Ossa. For the few weeks he had Nnanna in the house he had found him a lad of great promise, strong and bold and full of initiative. Nnanna's one great fault was that he was self-willed and pugnacious, prone to use his gift of strength to tyrannize over others; he would rather settle any serious disagreement with his fists. Just the week before, he had beaten Smart until Smart cried like an animal. Without doubt, he was seriously provoked, for Smart has cussedly called him homeless wild one; but Joseph flogged him for starting the fight and breaking the report-first rule by which the school fraternity was governed. Since that day, Nnanna had not beaten Smart, or anybody again, although he had continued to brandish his fists.

Under the special care and guidance of a Reverend Father, reasoned Joseph, especially a young and very kind one like Father Smith, Nnanna would certainly grow up to become the pride of those who had seen to his upbringing. Joseph the teacher was of the type who took remarkable interest in the future of their pupils. Some people said of him that he expiated a flight from parenthood, for he was still a bachelor. Some held that his motive was not all that altruistic; that he was out to seek vicarious status from his successful products.

After lunch the following day, he called Nnanna and said:

'Do you know you will leave for Ossa tomorrow?'

'Sa-ah!' Nnanna exclaimed joyously and his jaws parted.

'Yes, you will,' he went on in a dignified tone. 'Father will leave tomorrow and you will go with him. I want you to visit your mother before your departure.'

'Yes, Master.'

'You had better go immediately you've had your lunch. Just tell her,' he said gravely, 'that you are going away. Don't ask for her consent or you may not get it.'

'Yes, Master.'

'And make her understand that you are very happy to go to Ossa.'

'Yes, Master.'

'Come back immediately you've seen her.'

'I will, Master,' Nnanna promised.

On his way he called to see Ibe.

'Master says I shall leave tomorrow with Fada,' he announced gleefully.

Ibe's immediate reaction was to stare at him in confusion.

'Where to?'

'To Ossa.'

'Shut up!' Ibe said mechanically.

148

'It's true,' he affirmed. 'Master spoke to Fada yesterday and Fada agreed. I'm going into town now to tell Mother.'

Silence. 'So you are serious?'

'Am I serious? But I told you right from the start.'

'Well!' grunted Ibe fatalistically.

'So you didn't think I was serious all this time?'

'I don't know,' Ibe answered wearily; then paused. 'I believed you and I didn't.'

They were silent again.

'Let's go together and inform mother.'

Ibe blinked heavily, like an upright citizen called upon to abet evil. But Nnanna persisted. It took almost half an hour before he could convince Ibe to go with him. Even then, Ibe went reluctantly.

Okere's house was situated at the farther end of the town. They took advantage of the distance to work out a plan of action.

On arrival, they met her alone in the house, about to begin her lunch. They greeted her. She responded coldly and faced her meal.

'Mother,' Nnanna spoke, 'I've come to tell you that Fada has agreed to take me, and that we will leave tomorrow.'

She raised her face slowly and peered at him. 'What did you say?'

Ibe came in: 'Fada will take Nnanna—'

'Shut up, you!' she interrupted, frowning. 'Did anybody ask you to speak?'

Ibe grinned complacently.

'It's the thing Master told you about,' Nnanna resumed. He spoke elatedly, according to plan. 'Fada came the day before yesterday and we shall leave tomorrow.'

'You will leave for where?'

'For Ossa,' said Ibe. 'Nnanna is the only one chosen among the whole lot of us. How I wish I were chosen!'

'Corrupter!' she answered him.

'It's true,' Ibe went on, undaunted. 'How I wish I were in your place, Nnanna!'

She had begun to find his levity both amusing and irritating. She said:

'But didn't I ask you never to enter my house again, Ibe?'

'The one about mortar and knife, is it?' replied Ibe good-naturedly. 'I shall continue to visit you until you begin to like me again.'

Chiaku conceded a laugh. It was brief and inhibited and it terminated in a sigh of resignation. Then she proceeded with her lunch.

'How I envy you, Nnanna!' Ibe spoke again. 'One day you will return to Nade a big man.'

'Left to you, you would lead him right into a lion's den,' she accused.

'Not so, Mother,' Nnanna promptly corrected. 'I am very fortunate to be the only one chosen to go.'

She looked at them, from one to the other. She sobbed.

'I've no time this afternoon for foolish talks,' she said. 'Go to any place you like and leave me alone, please. Let the man take you away. He has already removed the kernel; let him now remove the shell.'

They communicated with their eyes, recording the beginning of success.

'But this Ossa you talk about, is it not the place where the old eat the liver of the young?'

'That's mere story,' Nnanna retorted.

'How I wish I could come with you, Nnanna,' Ibe said, still according to plan.

She rose, went into the middle room and brought an empty pot. She sat down, put the pot beside her and continued with her meal.

'By this time tomorrow we shall be on our way,' Nnanna said. 'I shall remember you from there, Mother.'

'Me? Why remember me after letting loose the swarm of bees that stung me for years on end? Don't; I have no need for that.'

Ibe changed the subject: 'You will be coming to see us from time to time, won't you, Nnanna?'

'It will depend on Fada,' he said. 'If he allows me I'll come. Or perhaps, I shall come with him whenever he visits Nade.'

'See that you inform Amanze, your father's brother,' she said harshly. 'And Oji too. I personally don't care any more.'

'I won't have the time to go and tell them. Please do that for me.'

'Why not! You want people to start saying that Chiaku has sold you to a stranger?' She paused. 'You like some of the food?'

'Thank you, we shall eat.' Ibe accepted promptly and advanced, smiling.

Into the empty pot Chiaku spooned the greater part of what was left of her meal and passed it to them.

'Those people must be kind indeed,' she remarked in a low, candid tone. 'See how that man has been caring for you for nearly a moon. And now, the white man comes to take you.'

They exchanged glances.

'But of course they started it all. It was they who lit the fire that burnt down my house.'

'So you still talk like that, Mother?' Nnanna asked.

'I expect to see you in the church one of these days,' Ibe added.

'May your tongue be glued to your palate, villain!' she cursed. 'Why don't you two go away now? I see you have finished your food. Go away and leave Chiaku to settle down here in peace. Do you know if this one I have in my womb will be a boy?'

'Come and see me before I leave,' Nnanna requested.

'Why not? I will even sleep inside that building in which you people assemble. Go away now and don't say more foolish things.'

'Let's go, Nnanna,' Ibe said. 'Master will be annoyed with us for over-staying.'

'True.'

They breezed out.

It was mid-morning. Chiaku was alone in the house. Oji came in.

He looked rather funny today, with his big eyelids painted white and yellow chalk marks on his rich breast muscles. From the bag which hung down his shoulder, he took out a roll of animal skin spotted white and black, spread it on the floor, and sat down on it in the fashion of a priest-doctor.

'My brother, when did that start?' she asked in her surprise.

'What?'

'I mean, when did you become a dibia?'

'I am not one yet,' he drawled; 'I am only starting to be.'

'At your age?'

'Why not? Is it ever too late to begin to serve the gods?'

'You are serious then?'

'You started and I replied. Or weren't you serious when you asked?' He shifted clumsily. 'I am very serious, my sister.'

'And what prompted it?'

'I'm glad you've asked,' he said solemnly. 'After seeing what Ezedibia did for us, I decided that I too should serve in my own humble way.'

Her eyes squinted.

'Ezedibia?'

'Yes, my sister. Ezedibia is great. He has done wonders for Oji and his one and only sister.'

'How could you say that when—' She winced.

'Hm!' he grunted. 'One day perhaps, you will get to know everything.'

She pondered the statement. She found no light. She asked instead:

'Did you see Nnanna yesterday?'

'I did. I was with Idimogu in the market square when he and Ibe were going back from here.'

'Did he tell you?'

He paused. 'He did. I'm sure they must have left for Ossa by now.'

'So I think. What is your feeling about it?'

'Oh, let him go,' he said thoughtfully. 'The journey which has a beginning must have an end, for him whose chi is awake. One day we shall hear his story. I'm more interested at the moment in what Ezedibia has done for us. Any bit of doubt that might have been left about it was removed when your son went away.'

'You speak to your sister in proverb!'

'It's plain language. I'm so happy you've come out of it safe. We shall sacrifice to the gods – to Igwe in particular; and we shall sacrifice to your chi. I'm arranging for that already. All that I require from you is a white-feathered cock. Tell Okere and ask him to go at once and thank Ezedibia than whom there's none greater.'

Till his death, Oji maintained that Nnanna's departure was part of Ezedibia's scheme of things.